I0760829

ÉLODIE DUQUETTE

Also by Simon Trowbridge

The Rise and Fall of the Royal Shakespeare Company

The Comédie-Française from Molière to Éric Ruf

Rameau

The Company

ÉLODIE DUQUETTE

A NOVEL

SIMON
TROWBRIDGE

ENGLANCE PRESS

First published by Englance Press, Oxford, in 2020
Revised impression, 2023

ISBN 978-1-9997305-4-3

Life can be magnificent and overwhelming, that is its whole tragedy. Without beauty, love or danger it would be almost easy to live.

ALBERT CAMUS

PART ONE

1

THE ONLY PASSENGER left on the station concourse was a young woman sitting on a suitcase.

'Lieutenant Duquette?'

'Yes.'

'Welcome to York. I'm Detective Sergeant Kevin Rose.'

They shook hands. 'I'm sorry it's so late,' she said. 'There was a long delay.'

'I'm sorry I walked right by you. I was expecting someone older.' This attractive woman in a short linen dress and sandals was the least likely detective he had ever seen.

His car was parked at the main entrance. As he drove down the hill and through Micklegate Bar he was tempted to use the siren to clear the traffic but thought better of it. Élodie rolled down the window. 'It's lovely tonight,' she said.

'Have you been travelling all day?'

‘Yes. The TGV to Paris, then the Eurostar, then…’

‘Then the trouble started.’

‘No, not at all. I love trains. What are the plans for tomorrow?’

‘I’ll pick you up eight. There’s a briefing at eight thirty.’

‘I have to see her parents in the afternoon.’

‘Yes. When we get to the hotel the DCI will be there. He wants to welcome you. A drink in the bar if that’s okay?’

‘Oh sorry, I should have said straight away. I have a place to stay. A friend is letting me use her flat. It’s near here.’

They were crossing Ouse Bridge. Groups of young people were making their way to the bars and clubs; holidaying families and couples were looking for restaurants and theatres. Walls of stone rose from the river to end in terraces of light and music. Élodie took in the parade of teenage girls and boisterous boys drinking beer from cans.

‘You know York?’

‘Yes. I spent a year working as an au pair in Scarborough and then I lived here for a while.’

‘Well, the chief is waiting in the foyer of the Novotel Hotel. I guess we shouldn’t leave him there.’

‘Could you ring him?’

‘Or we could go to the hotel and then I’ll drive you to the flat?’

‘Okay. What’s he like?’

‘Old school. Can we speak French? I’d like to practice.’

‘No. If you come to Bordeaux then we’ll speak French. It’s only fair.’

He smiled at her. 'But you don't need to practice.'

'Not true. Already I'm learning new phrases.'

She was looking out at the turreted city wall. He turned into the forecourt of the hotel and parked. She pulled down the mirror and tidied a few strands of hair that had fallen across her face. 'I'm a little nervous, and fatigued. I hope he's not a big drinker. Will he think I'm dressed inappropriately? I wasn't expecting to meet him tonight.'

'Don't worry.'

Chief Inspector Brown was pacing the bar. A large wavy-haired man in an old suit, he greeted Élodie warmly but with his habitual bluntness. 'We won't talk shop tonight. I just wanted to say how determined we all are to find this French girl. May I call you Élodie?'

'Of course. It was good of you to book me a room, but I'm staying at a friend's flat.' Conscious of her short dress she crossed her legs carefully.

'Well done, better than staying in this soulless place. A quick drink and then Rose will take you. What would you like?'

'Could I have a cup of tea?'

Brown paused. 'I'll join you.'

While Rose brought the drinks, Brown told Élodie, 'Cooperating with the French police is new territory for us so as we go along if you have any concerns of any kind just let me know. I have no truck with protocol. If you step on my toes and I shout at you don't take it to heart, I shout at everyone, and while you're with us I'll treat you as one of my team, if that's okay?'

'Yes, of course.'

'I wasn't expecting a slip of a girl.'

Élodie smiled. 'A slip of a girl?'

'If I forget myself and call you "lass" you shouldn't feel offended.'

'I'm not easily offended.'

•

The flat was in a converted warehouse at Queen's Staith. Élodie said goodnight to Rose and entered a minimally furnished apartment on the third floor. She stepped out onto the balcony and looked down at the dark water and then over Ouse Bridge to where the floodlit towers of the Minster jutted above the rooftops. On the opposite bank, people were sitting at tables outside the pubs and restaurants; others were perched on the edge of the river wall, their legs dangling over the side. A red pleasure boat appeared through the central arch of the bridge, its lights slashing across the water, followed by a chorus of laughter and music.

Élodie unpacked her suitcase in the bedroom and then took a quick shower. She walked from room to room, allowing the warm night air to dry her skin and leaving a trail of wet footprints across the floorboards. Her phone bleeped and she sighed as she noticed her boss's name on the display.

'Yes, capitaine?'

'Have you arrived?'

'Yes.'

'Have you met capitaine Brown?'

'Yes.'

'He sounded like a right bore on the phone.'

'He's fine.'

'Don't take any shit, okay?'

'Okay.'

'Are you all set for the meeting with Monsieur and Madame Roche tomorrow?'

'Yes.'

'They're breathing down the commissaire's neck and he's breathing down mine. Make sure you're courteous. Say the right things.'

'Yes.'

'Call me tomorrow. And email a report.'

'I will.'

Élodie dressed, left the flat and strolled across the bridge to the opposite quay. She turned into a cobbled lane that climbed away from the river, and in through the blue framed entrance of a restaurant. Thirteen years before she had spent the final months of her year in England waitressing here. The restaurant was no longer the old-style brasserie of her memory. It had been modernised and expensively redecorated. The waitresses, though, still wore the same black skirts and red aprons. She asked to see the owner, Raymond Pariselle. A waitress pointed at the stairs and Élodie climbed to the second floor, a long rectangular space overlooking the river.

Raymond's hair was blacker than she remembered, but he wore the same combination of tailored blue suit and brown Oxford brogues. She watched for a few moments as he chided a waitress, his largely incomprehensible English lapsing into French. The girl shrugged.

When Raymond recognised Élodie he lifted her off the ground for a few seconds. 'Ma petite, you are just the same! Why are you here? Do you want a job?'

She smiled. 'I have a job. I'm a police officer.'

'That's ridiculous.'

'I did write and tell you.'

'Well, I chose not to believe it.' He frowned. 'What a tragedy. Who will marry you now?'

He led her to a secluded table by the window. 'Are you hungry?'

'Only a little. Something light. An omelette?'

'Are you sure?'

'Yes.'

He called over a waitress and placed the order. 'Quickly please, Anna. And a bottle of Château Minuty.'

'Oui, maître.'

The restaurant was closing and only a few customers remained. Raymond lit a cigar. 'Why have you returned to York?'

'A French girl is missing. Laura Roche. Do you know her?'

'Of course. As you predicted.'

She smiled. 'There aren't that many French people in York and this is the best French restaurant.'

'She worked here for a few weeks.'

'And…?'

'You need to talk to Anna, one of my English girls. They were friends.'

Raymond called Anna over, made the introductions and offered her a chair. He took the bottle of rosé from the wine waiter and filled three glasses.

'Do you mind talking to me about Laura?'

'No, I guess not.'

'How did you meet her?'

'On the Eurostar. She told me that she was working for a family in London but was looking for something else. We exchanged addresses and a few weeks later she turned up in York. There was a spare room in the house I share so she moved in. I got her a job here.'

'What is she like?'

'At first I liked her.' Anna paused.

'Did something happen?'

'Laura slept with the boyfriend of one of my flatmates. It wasn't a big deal, but I was embarrassed and angry.'

'So, you fell out?'

'It wasn't as if we were great friends, was it? We'd only known each other a few weeks. She moved in with the boy, stopped working here and from then on we tried to avoid each other.'

'When did you last see her?'

'I don't know. At a party I think, about a month ago.'

'Can you give me the names of the people you've just mentioned?'

'I suppose.'

'The Yorkshire police will probably ask you to make a formal statement.'

She nodded, writing the names on a napkin. 'Now can I go?'

'Yes.'

Anna finished her glass of wine. Another girl arrived with the omelette, a green salad and a basket of bread. Raymond said, 'Now I believe that you're a flic. I must work, but when you've finished eating we'll have a coffee.'

Élodie looked out of the window. Along the river the lights were going out and the crowds had dispersed to leave only the few and the solitary – a couple sitting together at the stern of a barge, their cigarettes occasionally glowing red; two youths riding a scooter along the quay; a woman sitting alone on a bus speeding over the bridge. A breeze had gathered, and in the gardens downstream the trees were swaying. Élodie was too tired to eat. She curled up on the leather chair and closed her eyes.

•

Rose was almost home when the call came over the police radio. He turned the car round in the quiet suburban street and sped through the nocturnal city to the meadows at Fulford. Ahead, across the dark windswept field, he could see his destination: an area guarded by police vehicles and illuminated by portable lights.

In daylight this meadow formed a small park beside the river. For Rose, who often went jogging here, it would never be the same. He ducked under the perimeter tape and walked over to where DI Tom Gould was leaning against a patrol car with his back to the crime scene. Rose was not surprised to see the white leads of an iPhone dangling from Gould's ears for he had come to realise that the inspector turned to classical music at times of stress.

The two detectives nodded a greeting and walked in silence to where the body of a young woman lay between the tall riverside trees. 'Fits the description of the missing French girl,' Gould said. 'Dark hair, early twenties. No ID on her; no obvious sign of injury or foul play. Two boys saw her in the river and pulled her up the bank. Not dead that long I'd say. I don't need to take another a look but see what you think.'

The girl was wearing jeans and a T-shirt sodden by water and blackened by mud. Her feet were bare. Rose forced himself to look at her face, but discovered, as usual, that the face of a corpse gave away little sense of the living person. It was the girl's toes that caused him to shiver.

'Could be Laura.'

'Check the labels on her clothes. If they're French we'll know.'

Rose carefully moved her head to one side and looked inside the top. He similarly checked the jeans and underwear. 'All in English.'

'Inconclusive then.'

Across the river a small crowd of onlookers had gathered. Gould turned to one of the uniformed officers. 'Get someone over there. Quietly. I want their names and addresses. Arrest anyone who tries to run away.'

They heard a car pull to a halt and a few moments later DCI Brown stepped into the light.

Gould said, 'A young woman, sir.'

Brown walked over to the body but returned almost at once. 'The French girl?'

'There's nothing to identify her as French, but it looks likely,' Gould said.

'Where's the pathologist?'

'He's on his way.'

'Who found the body?'

'Two lads. They were riding along the towpath on a scooter.'

The two boys were sitting on the back seat of a police car. Brown opened the door and inserted his big head into the cabin. He addressed the younger, a boy of about sixteen. 'Tell me what happened.'

'We saw her in the water. We pulled her out but she was dead.'

Brown nodded. 'You did the right thing, lad. If she'd been alive you might have saved her. Did you find a bag or wallet?'

'No.'

'Anyone else about?'

'No, it was quiet.'

'No one on the opposite bank?'

'No.'

'Is that right?' Brown asked the other boy.

'Yes.'

'Which way did you come from?'

'From town.'

'All along the river?'

'Yes.'

'Meet anyone on the way, running or in a hurry or looking agitated?'

'No.'

'How long before you called 999?'

'A few minutes.'

'Good.'

The pathologist had arrived and was leaning over the body. Brown knew that it was best to leave him alone until he was ready to speak. Brown noticed Gould's iPhone.

'What have you been listening to?'

Gould was reluctant to answer, but then remembered that Brown sang in a choir. 'Byrd. The motet Ne irascaris Domine.'

'Ah yes, "Be not so very angry, Lord, and remember not our iniquity forever". Are you a Catholic, Tom?'

'No.'

The pathologist came over. 'First thoughts are that she drowned.'

'Tell me something I don't know.'

'No sign of any physical assault.'

'Time of death?'

'She hadn't been in the water for very long, probably for no longer than thirty minutes.'

'Anything else?'

'No. Of course, this is all unconfirmed until I get her on the table.'

Brown grimaced. 'Don't let me keep you.'

2

Rose collected Élodie at eight. 'We've found the body of a girl.' He looked at the bog brown water of the Ouse. 'She drowned in the river last night.'

Her heart sank. 'Is it her?'

'No I/D, but the right age and hair colour.'

'Clothes?'

'Yes. English labels.'

At headquarters, members of Brown's squad were gathering in the incident room on the second floor. Officers leant against the edges of desks or stood restlessly.

Brown called for silence. 'Okay, welcome to lieutenant Duquette of the Bordeaux police. Lieutenant is equivalent to our DI. I know because I've just looked it up on the Internet.' He turned to the only female member of his team, a young woman with strawberry blonde hair. 'Off you go, Karen.'

‘First report from the pathologist, sir, confirms that the girl drowned. No evidence of violence or sexual assault. A small tattoo of a scorpion on her right foot.’

‘Are there any other missing girls that we know about?’ Gould asked.

‘None locally fitting the age and description.’

‘For the purposes of this session, let’s assume that the girl isn’t Laura,’ Brown said.

He asked Élodie to say something about Laura’s family.

‘The father, Charles Roche, is a businessman, a very influential figure in Bordeaux. He’s a property developer, but also owns vineyards and restaurants. He has indicated to my chief that it is not out of character for Laura to go missing. He wants a discreet approach at present.’

Brown said, ‘Yes, he said the same to me, and I’ll follow his wishes up to a point, depending on where we are.’

‘What about the mother?’ Gould asked.

‘I’ve yet to have any contact with her. She was an actress when she was young. She appeared in plays by Shakespeare and Racine during the 1970s.’

‘I met her yesterday,’ Brown said. ‘She didn’t say a word. Is Roche connected?’

‘Connected?’

‘Politically.’

‘Yes. Very much.’

‘Is this going to become a circus? Is he known to the general public?'

'No.'

'But his wife is known, surely?' Karen said.

'No. She retired from acting a long time ago, and she never had a film or television career.'

'That won't stop the press,' Rose said. 'There'll be headlines like "Actress's Daughter Missing".'

'We don't have that kind of newspaper in France,' Élodie said.

'We're not in France,' Rose said.

'What do we know about Laura?' Brown asked Élodie.

'We've yet to start investigating her life in France. What we know is that before she came to England she was studying at Aix-en-Provence University. She dropped out in her second year. There's another daughter, Camille. She's currently a graduate student at Oxford. Last month Laura visited her parents in Bordeaux and also went to Aix to see some friends. We know she caught the Eurostar to return to England early on the morning of Sunday 15 June.'

'Later that day,' Karen said, looking at Élodie, 'we're assuming she returned to York by train because she bought a ticket with her credit card. The other residents in the apartment block where she lives haven't been able to help. It seems people keep to themselves. She was expected at the cinema café where she works on the Monday but never showed. She wasn't reported as missing until her mother tried to ring her three weeks later.'

'Last night I spoke to a girl who explained how Laura came to

York,' Élodie said. She told them about the restaurant and the waitress called Anna.

There was a tense silence. Brown glared at Karen. 'How did you miss this?'

'We've only just started, sir.'

'Right. Slow starters, aren't we? Go to this restaurant and interview the staff.'

'Yes.' She looked accusingly at Élodie.

Brown ended the meeting and called Élodie and Gould into his office. 'You have no jurisdiction to investigate here. Defence lawyers will shit all over us. I shouldn't have to make that clear.'

'Of course. It was an opportunity that came up. I didn't mean to get anyone into trouble.'

'Best if you two team up. Élodie, I want you to come with me to see the parents. I'm going to ask them to view the body.'

'I don't know…'

'If it is their daughter the sooner they know the better.'

•

Élodie stood to one side as Brown greeted Charles Roche. They had just entered the Roches' hotel suite. The large Georgian room overlooked a quiet treelined street. Through an open door Élodie could see a fourposter bed. Charles Roche wore a blue pinstriped suit and a red tie. His tall bearing and azure eyes compelled attention. His wife, Elisabeth, was sitting on a settee.

'This is lieutenant Duquette.'

Élodie came forward. Roche offered his hand in cursory acknowledgement. She stepped back.

'I know you were expecting to see lieutenant Duquette this afternoon, but something has come up.' Brown placed his hand on Roche's arm and kept it there. 'It may not be Laura, but the body of a girl has been found in the river.'

Roche nodded. 'When?'

'Last night. I'm so sorry to put you through this.'

'Take me to see her.'

'We'll go together,' his wife said.

'No. Will you give me a moment with my wife, Chief Inspector? I'll meet you downstairs in a few minutes.'

No one spoke during the short car journey or the desolate procession down the morgue's long corridors. As the girl's face was revealed, Roche kept his feelings locked inside. He simply shook his head and said, 'She's not Laura.'

Outside, though, he lit a cigar and his manner seemed less severe. He called his wife. Brown and Élodie leant against the car and waited. 'He was very calm,' Élodie said.

'Let's take him to the station for your meeting, if he agrees. Gould can then sit in.'

'I don't know.'

'I noticed the way he was with you.'

She shrugged. 'It's not a problem.'

'If he has something relevant to say about his daughter's

disappearance, and I'm guessing he has, Gould will be freer than you to ask the awkward questions. I sense you're in a difficult position.'

'I wanted to talk to both parents.'

'He's not going to let his wife say anything, is he? Better to speak to her when she's on her own.'

Roche agreed to go to the station. Élodie, to make sure, told him that she was happy to stick to the original plan. 'No, this is better,' he said irritably. 'It means my wife won't be disturbed.'

At the station, Brown arranged for coffee to be brought to the meeting room. He introduced Gould to Roche and then withdrew. 'Capitaine Bercot told me to offer you any assistance,' Élodie said in French.

Roche placed his chair to the side of the table and crossed his legs. 'Bercot is overanxious,' he replied in impeccable English. 'I do not need anyone from home to hold my hand. My mother was English and I studied at Oxford. You should know this. However, it is perfectly sensible for the two police forces to work together, and I support that. Bercot speaks highly of you, as does Brown after only a few hours. So I will ask Bercot to let you get on with it. Will that help?'

'Yes, it will.'

Gould said: 'We know that your daughter dropped out of university before coming to England…?'

'Yes. Without my knowledge. She didn't want to study at Oxford or one of the grandes écoles but deliberately chose a second-rate university as far away from Paris as possible. One day she phoned to say she had left Aix and was working in London as an au pair. Laura has a rebellious streak, Inspector. She can be wilful in the extreme.'

'Did she break up with a boy?' Gould asked.

'She wouldn't give an explanation.'

'Is Laura estranged from her family?'

The question irritated Roche. 'When a daughter grows up she becomes difficult. I expect she'll show up soon. When she wants money, I'll get a phone call.'

'We'd like to publicise her disappearance,' Gould said.

'If she knows we're looking for her you may get that phone call,' Élodie said.

'I feel it's too early to go public. Brown and Bercot agree.'

'Can you let us know the name of the family she worked for in London?'

'My secretary will know.'

'Your other daughter is at Oxford?'

'Yes, she's at my old college. I'd rather you left her alone. I've spoken to her, of course, and she hasn't heard from Laura.'

They spoke for ten or so more minutes. As he was leaving Roche said to Élodie, 'I'd like you to ring me every day with an update. I'll be in contact with your boss as well of course.' He looked at her. She was wearing a black suit and a white blouse, her hair tied up. Self-conscious, she touched her hair. 'You look like one of my secretaries. I'm impressed. They receive a clothes allowance that I imagine is more than your salary.'

Élodie forced a smile.

•

Gould and Élodie spent the rest of the day tracing Laura's life in the city. They started by going to her flat in an apartment block overlooking the Foss. The redbrick building was in a poor state of repair. There was no communal garden; no concierge. Inside Laura's ground floor flat the rooms were clean and uncluttered. The bed was made. Designer dresses and expensive shoes filled the small wardrobe. Bottles of perfume and items of makeup were arranged neatly on the dressing table.

'I don't like this part,' Élodie said.

Gould retreated to the living room and looked at the small collection of books and CDs that occupied the single bookcase. 'She had good taste,' he called.

'Has good taste.'

'Her books are mostly literary. Rimbaud, Flaubert, Dickens, D.H. Lawrence, Camus, Virginia Woolf.... Very little light reading here. Agatha Christie.'

'She studied literature at university.'

'She likes the Beatles, the Who, Gainsbourg, Radiohead, Miles Davies, but also Bach, Puccini, Mahler... It's an unusual collection for a twenty-one-year-old.'

Élodie joined Gould in the living room. 'Why?'

'You don't think so?'

'Do you think it belongs to someone else?'

'No. She's signed her name in all the books.'

He passed her Laura's dogeared paperback of Rimbaud's poems. On the frontispiece she had scribbled her name followed by 'aged 17'. Élodie flipped through the pages. 'She's marked the poem Roman.' He looked over her shoulder and read the first stanza.

On n'est pas sérieux, quand on a dix-sept ans.
Un beau soir, foin des bocks et de la limonade,
Des cafés tapageurs aux lustres éclatants!
On va sous les tilleuls verts de la promenade.

'No one's serious when they're seventeen?'

'Yes. Do you know it?'

'No.'

'We all study it at school.'

Élodie closed the book and placed it back on the shelf.

'I don't think she ever got home the day she returned to York,' Gould said. 'There are no suitcases or bags here.'

Élodie continued his line of thought. 'No laptop or iPad. In fact, there's nothing personal here. Notebooks, diary, photo albums, letters…'

'Young people keep all that stuff online these days,' Gould said.

'Do we know if she is on Facebook or Twitter?'

Gould phoned Karen and activated speaker mode. 'Is Laura on

Facebook or anything similar?'

'I don't think so.'

'What does that mean?'

'It means that if she is, she's not using her real name.'

'Have we taken anything away from her flat?'

'It's as she left it, sir.'

'Okay. Thanks.'

Gould and Élodie walked into the small kitchen. 'We're not learning much, are we?' Élodie said.

'She's enigmatic, don't you think?'

'In the sense that she's missing, yes, but otherwise… I don't know. I think someone else has been here. It's too clean and tidy.'

'There's basic CCTV outside but unfortunately it hasn't been working for months.'

They returned to Gould's car and drove the short distance to the cinema on Coney Street. In the café Élodie, who liked to get a sense of people before questioning them, said to Gould, 'Let's wait before revealing who we are.' They sat at a table and ordered two coffees.

Framed posters of famous art films of the 1960s decorated one wall; photographs of their directors another. Glass doors gave out onto a terrace overlooking the Ouse. Behind the counter a man in his thirties wearing sunglasses was chatting to a waitress.

When they finally asked to see the manager it was the young man who walked over. Gould told him to remove the glasses. 'Why didn't you report Laura Roche as missing?'

'I didn't know she was missing. I thought she'd decided to leave.'

'When did you last hear from her?'

'Some weeks ago, when she returned from France. She phoned to say she was back in York and would come to work in the morning. She didn't turn up.'

'You didn't think it was strange that she left without collecting her final salary payment?' Élodie asked.

'Not really. She was absent-minded.'

'So you weren't unhappy to see her go?'

'Honestly, no.'

'How did she get on with the other members of staff?'

'All right. The not turning up was a problem. The bored attitude. The other girls weren't particularly tolerant of her.'

'And you?' Élodie asked.

'All right.'

'Was she close to anyone here?'

'No.'

'Do you know if she had a boyfriend?'

'A guy called for her a number of times. He works on the boats.'

He led them out to the edge of the terrace. A pleasure boat was docking. 'That's him, in the cabin.'

Gould and Élodie went down to the quay and joined the queue of people waiting to board the boat. 'Can we take the trip?' Élodie asked. 'Do you mind?'

He did, but didn't say so.

'It's not long,' she said, sensing it.

They spent forty minutes on the open top deck while the young man both piloted the vessel and delivered a tourist commentary in a manner that was dull and methodical and occasionally incomprehensible. At the end of the cruise Élodie told him that she had enjoyed his talk and he showed both surprise and pleasure until Gould took out his warrant card. They instructed him to sit with them on the otherwise vacated deck.

'I wondered who you were. Thought you were from the company, checking up on me.'

Gould left a pause. 'What's your name?'

'Michael Scott.'

'Laura Roche. She's your girlfriend, right?'

'No, not really.'

'Are you worried about her?'

'No. Should I be?'

'Do you know where she is?'

'No. Listen, I saw her on and off, that's all. I don't know what I was to her. Not a boyfriend. We were never a couple.'

'But she moved in with you?'

'That was at the start of our thing. Just for a week or so while she found her own flat.'

'Were you upset when she left?' Élodie asked.

'Yes. I liked her. She was out of my league; I always knew that.'

'How did you meet her?'

'She moved into the house where my girlfriend at the time lived.

My girlfriend caught us kissing and that was that.'

'Do you think Laura set out to wreck your relationship?'

'No. She was drunk and unhappy and I made a clumsy pass. My girlfriend walked in, misunderstood and unleashed the dogs of war… The other girls ganged up on Laura and threw her out. She had nowhere to live. That was the only reason she went with me. As I said, she found her own place within weeks.'

'Did Laura ever confide in you about the things that were going on in her life?'

'No.'

'You said just now that she was unhappy.'

'That's how she seemed to me. Listen, what's happened to her? Why are you asking me these questions?'

'She's missing.'

'Were you pestering her?' Gould asked. 'You asked to see her at the cinema café where she works.'

'Everyone goes to the cinema café. I asked after her just to say hello.'

'Where were you on Sunday 15 June?'

'Is this for real? Are you accusing me of harming Laura?'

'We're not accusing you. Where were you on 15 June?'

Michael reached for his phone. 'I was on holiday. In Spain.'

'Thank you for talking to us,' Élodie said. 'If you think of anything else that might help us please ring the station.'

'Of course. I hope she's okay. You should talk to the guy who runs the café.'

•

Élodie asked the desk sergeant for a car and the next morning, a Saturday, drove to Scarborough to visit the couple she had worked for when she was eighteen. They had kept in touch, and had met a few times in London and Bordeaux, but this was the first time that Élodie had returned to the spacious three storey house where, as a teenager, she had looked after their two daughters (the narrow stairs and creaky wooden floors and unexpected windows with views of the sea provoked happy memories of scattered toys, children's laughter and an old spaniel spraying her legs with rainwater). After lunch she braved the cold water of the grey North Sea.

On the Sunday she set out for Brown's home in the countryside south of York. He had invited her to lunch (handing her a scribbled map) before leaving on Friday. His home turned out to be an isolated farmhouse on a hillside of small cornfields and copses at the end of a chalk track. She feared she was lost until she saw the name of his house on a gatepost. She parked beside a derelict barn and entered an apple orchard. Here she came across a girl of about fifteen, leaning against a tree. Beyond, in a meadow of long grass, there was a grey horse. The girl was smoking a cigarette.

'Are you the French policewoman?'

'Yes. Élodie.'

'I'm Maud. Don't tell him you caught me having a fag.'

'Is that your horse?'

'Yes.' They heard an engine and turned to see a boy on a motorbike entering the yard. The girl waved excitedly. 'I have to go. Tell them I've gone into town.' She ran away between the trees.

The front door was open, the house seemingly empty. Élodie walked through the old rooms to the back garden. Brown was reading the papers.

'There you are,' he said.

'Your daughter's gone into town.'

'I heard the bike.'

'She's very pretty.'

'My wife's gone ahead. We should go.'

'Aren't we having lunch?'

'There'll be plenty to eat at the match.'

'The match?'

'Cricket. It's Sunday. You don't mind a short walk to the village?'

'No, of course not.'

Brown led Élodie across the meadow. A narrow path cut through a cornfield and up the slope of a hill. There wasn't enough room to walk side by side. Brown marched ahead in his cricket whites. 'Everything all right?'

'Yes, all right.'

'Gould and some of the others will be there. We'll talk together later.'

'I need to be back in Bordeaux by Wednesday.'

'Your boss told me.'

'I'll come back though.'

'If he lets you. The latest is that the father wants us to back off. Says she'll turn up when she's good and ready. What are you going to tell Bercot when you get back?'

'That I don't think she's going to turn up.'

He stopped for a moment to look at her. The path had almost disappeared. They were standing waist deep in the corn beneath a pylon. Brown tried to see Élodie's eyes through her sunglasses. Her summer dress was covered in pollen dust and grass seeds. He sensed her discomfort. 'What makes you think that?'

'What we've learnt is that she's… high maintenance. She makes use of people. She doesn't seem the type to go off on her own. It's just an instinct at this point; there's no acceptable evidence to back it up.'

'She could have gone off with someone else.' He walked on.

'Yes, a boy, that's possible. But she doesn't seem to stick with anyone for very long.'

'Bercot says he's thinking of coming over. He knows he's powerless but thinks he can influence my decision.'

'You're wrong if you think he's going to do whatever Monsieur Roche wants. He's a good officer.'

'Well, that's very loyal of you.'

They had reached the trees at the brow of the hill, and from there a sunken lane led down into the village.

The cricket pitch was circular, slightly sloping and only separated from the cornfields by a row of tall chestnut trees and a narrow stretch of scrub. There was a small wooden pavilion with a clock, a red post box and an old metal roller.

Élodie sat on a deck chair beside Karen. 'It's the same old story,' Karen said. 'The men have all the fun and the women watch.'

Élodie, though, was happy to watch the game. Most of the women were chatting and paying scant attention to the players. When a batsman was dismissed a woman would momentarily look up as he walked by and make consoling comments like a mother talking to her child.

Brown's team were batting. Gould walked to the crease and was out lbw first ball.

'Bad luck,' Élodie said sympathetically. She liked to observe etiquette and was a quick learner.

'You were robbed, sir,' Karen said, laughing.

Over by the cars a couple were arguing. 'Listening to that makes me glad that I'm single,' Karen said. 'Are you married?'

'No. Is Tom?'

'Yes. His wife avoids these social occasions. I think they're having problems. Does anyone have a happy marriage in this job?'

Brown went in next and scored four sixes in his first over, the last of them clearing the trees and falling into the corn. A gang of boys pursued the ball on their bikes, lifting dust. Gould emerged from the pavilion and sat on the grass beside Élodie's legs. 'The boss had a trial for Yorkshire when he was a schoolboy, could have played professionally.'

Karen leant across to tell Gould, 'The bowler's about twelve!'

She started to laugh again.

'Listen, Karen…' Gould lunged at her playfully and she ran away. He caught up and tackled her down in the long grass, pinning her arms back.

'You like her, don't you?' Karen said.

'Who?'

'Who? Really? Élodie.'

'No, not especially.'

'Sitting with your mouth an inch away from her bare thighs. Let me go. I said let me go.'

She kicked herself free. They walked back to the deck chairs. Élodie was finishing talking to someone on her phone. 'Roche.'

'What's happened?'

'Nothing. He rang to complain that you've been bullying his secretary.'

'I asked her to give details of the people Laura was working for in London. And also contact information for his other daughter. You've agreed that we need to interview the sister.'

'Yes, but I can't say that to the father. Did his secretary tell you?'

'No. Karen's found out anyway.'

'Jeremy Brenton,' Karen said.

'He's a civil servant,' Gould said.

'No, he's a government adviser.'

'What's the difference?'

'He's a spin doctor. Even turns up on TV occasionally.'

Brown hit a four and then ran a quick single to keep the strike.

'And the sister?'

'She's at New College,' Karen said.

Storm clouds had been gathering for some time, their shadows drifting over the fields. There was a rumble of thunder and rain fell. Everyone ran to shelter in the pavilion. Tea was served. The storm passed, but the field, awash with water, prevented any further play. The cricketers shook hands and departed. Car engines started up and headlamp beams made the dusk seem darker. After a quick drink in the pub Brown invited Élodie back to his home for dinner. Mrs Brown was a kind and attentive hostess. She had read modern languages at university and had lived in Geneva during her student years. She banned all talk of both police work and cricket and cut her intimidating husband down to size in a gently humorous way.

3

As they approached St Pancras Élodie leant forward and said, 'How about if I come with you? I can catch a later train.'

'Yes, if you like,' Gould said. He turned around. 'I knew you were going to say that.'

Rose swerved the car to avoid a bus. They made slow progress along the Euston Road, and down into west London. The windows were open and noise and fumes clogged the air until they escaped into the shaded side streets and squares of a quarter of white townhouses and private gardens behind railings.

Their destination was one such house, part of a long terrace five storeys high. A servant asked them to wait in the spacious hall. At length, an unsmiling middle-aged woman appeared.

'Can I help you?' she said.

Gould showed her his warrant card and introduced the others. 'And you are?' he asked.

'I'm in charge here.'

'You're expecting us. We have an appointment to see Jeremy Brenton.'

'I'm afraid Mr Brenton is not here.'

'Where is he?'

She looked pointedly at her wristwatch. 'Mr Brenton's at work.'

'My office arranged this appointment.'

'Yes, well, it was on the understanding that Mr Brenton might not be available.'

'Is Mrs Brenton here?'

'No, I'm afraid she's out.'

'You were told that we needed to see both Mr and Mrs Brenton.'

'If available. I regret that there has been a misunderstanding.'

'Okay. We'll go to Scotland Yard to find out about this misunderstanding. However, I'm going to leave Sergeant Rose here to wait for Mrs Brenton's return. He can ring me as soon as that happens. And while he's here he'll interview you and anyone else here who knew Laura Roche.'

'That's not convenient,' she snapped.

'Are you refusing?'

'No, of course I'm not refusing. But I can't say when Mrs Brenton will be home, if at all.'

In the car, Élodie asked Gould, 'Are we really going to Scotland Yard?'

'No, we're going to Brenton's office. If I'd said that to her she would have been straight on the phone to tell him.'

‘Why are they hiding from us?’

‘I doubt it’s that. It makes them feel superior to get the police to run around like this. We’ll turn things to our advantage and get some fun out of it by turning up unexpectedly at the Treasury.’

They drove to Whitehall and parked near St James’s Park in sight of the Treasury building. The officials didn’t attempt to block their entrance, but the process took over half-an-hour. At length a beautiful young woman led them out of the dark echoing halls of the main building and into a modern annexe of pale colours, glass and light. The door to Brenton’s office was open and he was sitting in his shirtsleeves with his polished shoes on the glass surface of a desk that was bare except for an iPhone and a Mont Blanc fountain pen. The woman asked them to wait for a moment and went into the office. She placed her manicured fingers on Brenton’s shoulder and leant close to his face; as she turned her ponytail lightly caressed his skin.

The woman beckoned to Élodie and Gould and closed the door on leaving. Brenton smiled and offered his hand. In appearance he could have been a premier league football player of the lean, expensively groomed and besuited type – he had that kind of physicality and self-confidence. His accent, though, was top public school. They sat either side of a low coffee table.

‘We were expecting to see you at your house,’ Gould said.

‘I hope you haven’t been too put out. Shit happens.’

‘You know why we’re here. This is not a trivial matter.’

‘Of course. My assistant phoned to say that you’d left an officer to wait for my wife. I'm afraid my wife's away and won't be returning home today. My assistant also said that you were going to Scotland Yard and not coming here. That was fucking cheeky. By the way, do you have the permission of the Met to be operating here?'

'You could ring them and ask.'

Brenton paused. 'No, that won't be necessary. Let's get on with it.'

'Laura Roche was your au pair for a while. Is that right?'

'Yes.'

'When exactly?'

'From the 3rd of January to the 3rd of April this year.'

'Why did she leave?'

'I sacked her.'

'Why?'

'She was no good at the job. Simple as that. We decided to let her go after the probation period.'

'What happened?'

'Nothing in particular. She was lazy and disinterested, hopeless with the children and unwilling to do any task she considered to be outside the job description.'

'Can I ask why you employed her in the first place?' Élodie asked. 'What made you think she'd be good as an au pair?'

'My wife and housekeeper chose her.'

'Did she bring people back to the house? Was that a problem?'

'I'm sure she did, but that was never the issue.'

'How did she take to being sacked?' Gould asked.

'Very well. She knew it was coming.'

'Have you had any contact with her since?'

'Why would I? Charles thinks she'll turn up when she's ready. We could have had this little chat on the phone, Inspector.'

'You know her father?' Élodie said.

'Yes. Not at the time I employed her, more's the pity. We met for the first time this week. I naturally wanted to express my concern.' He looked at his watch. 'If there's nothing else...'

'If you could ask your wife to ring me when she returns home,' Gould said.

'My wife's not too well.'

'Nevertheless.'

Brenton nodded. He rose and held out his hand. 'Listen, while you're here you should visit the Cabinet War Rooms.'

The young woman had returned. She escorted them out of the building.

•

By the time Gould and Élodie had returned to Chelsea and picked up Rose it was late in the afternoon. Élodie rang Bordeaux to say that she was going to stay the night in London and Gould and Rose decided to do the same despite knowing that Brown wouldn't authorise a hotel on expenses, particularly a five-star boutique hotel in the Aldwych, which was where they ended up.

Gould and Rose waited in the bar for Élodie to join them for a drink before dinner. 'Did you get anything from Brenton's staff?' Gould asked.

'Nothing. The woman was astonishingly guarded and very good at it.'

Élodie stepped out of the lift. 'I've just had a call from Charles Roche,' she said. 'He's asked me to go over to his house.'

'He has a home in London?'

'Yes, I didn't know it.'

'How does he know you're here?'

'I don't know.'

'I hope you told him to fuck off,' Rose said.

'No, I should go. It won't take long.' She looked at Gould. 'Will you come with me?'

'Of course.'

'Sorry to be a pain. Do you mind waiting?' she asked Rose.

'No. I'll book a table for later.'

Gould asked the concierge to bring the car.

'Where are we going?'

'Bedford Square.'

Élodie was preoccupied during the short drive along Southampton Row to Bloomsbury. Gould parked the car in the square and they crossed the road not like police officers but like an attractive couple who weren't speaking. Roche opened the door himself and wasn't pleased to see Gould. He asked Gould to wait in the hall. Behind Roche's back, Élodie gestured that it was all right. Gould said, 'No problem.' Roche led Élodie into a sitting room and closed the door.

Table lamps illuminated the central part of the room, creating an area of light surrounded by near darkness. 'Why did you bring him?' Roche demanded, unable to hide his anger. He was around sixty-five, and yet his height and bearing and anger made him appear strong. In the lamplight his eyes were deep-set, his nose prominent, and the tension in his body was undisguised and predatory.

'Because I'm working closely with the English police and I thought…'

'Well, he can wait in the hall like a servant.'

Roche sat down and lit a cigar. On the coffee table there was an uncorked bottle of red wine and two large Bordeaux glasses. He pointed at the chair opposite. 'Sit down, Mademoiselle.'

Élodie obeyed. 'I'm sorry, there's no news, Monsieur Roche.'

'We'll get to that. Do you know anything about wine?'

'Not much. Nothing, actually. I like it.'

He filled both glasses. 'This is one of mine. From my estate in the Médoc.'

In the subdued light the wine looked black. Hiding her reluctance out of courtesy, Élodie reached for the glass and took a sip. 'It's delicious.'

'Delicious?'

'Yes.'

He was holding the stem of his glass and contemplating the

wine. He placed his nose over the rim but didn't drink. 'I envy you. A man drinks wine to feel close to the land, to history and culture. A woman drinks wine only for sensual pleasure, to satisfy an appetite.' He registered the look on her face and said, 'Of course, such a sexist attitude offends you, but you know it contains a truth. You have just admitted your own lack of interest in the science or culture of wine, and you're a Bordelaise. The taste and the way it makes you feel are enough. Now I can see that you're irritated because you've fallen into my little trap.'

'Not at all.'

She took another sip of wine. Roche was gently rolling the liquid in his glass.

'My daughters, when they were young, would join the pickers at harvest time. This is always a celebration, a process of hard work but also of enjoyment and companionship. Every year I bring young people together from France and England to work on the vineyard, two nations that have a shared history in the Gironde but an awkward relationship. Both girls worked hard, with dedication and a desire to learn. Then, one year, it was different. They had reached puberty and were more interested in the party atmosphere of this gathering of young people than in anything else. Camille still worked hard and had the obedience to allow me to bore her with my lectures, but Laura only came alive when she was with a group of boys. It was the first time she ran away. My wife slapped her for some reason and she disappeared for days. The beginning of a pattern.'

'But, if I've understood, Laura has never gone missing for this long before?'

'That's true. But she's an adult now. She can do what she likes.'

'I haven't yet been able to talk with Camille or your wife, Monsieur Roche. Is your wife here?'

'I think you know she's not here,' Roche said. He tasted the wine, retaining the liquid for several seconds in his mouth before swallowing. 'She's at home in Bordeaux.'

'I'm returning to Bordeaux tomorrow. Perhaps she would be willing to see me during the next few days?'

'I'll talk to my wife and daughter. If they want to meet with you then of course they can. But I won't have them pressured. Does that satisfy you?'

'I just want to do a good job.'

'Of course. Laura's rebellion embarrasses me. I don't want it to become a topic of conservation in Bordeaux. Do you understand?'

'Yes, I understand.'

For a moment Roche was silent, lost in thought. Élodie wanted to leave, so she emptied her glass quickly. She felt Roche's disapproval and his charisma, and her own susceptibility, and was glad she'd asked Gould along. She rose from the chair. 'If that's all... My colleague's waiting.'

'I planned to take you out to dinner.'

'Well, thank you, but that's not possible.'

'Not possible? Who do you think you are?'

'Please don't talk to me like that.'

'I'll talk to you how I like.'

'You're forgetting yourself, Monsieur Roche.'

He left another pause. 'You'd better go.'

The image of a schoolgirl leaving her headmaster's office came into Gould's mind as Élodie joined him in the hall, closing the door behind her. She looked unsteady on her feet so he took hold of her upper arm.

'My head's spinning a little. I had to drink a large glass of red wine.'

'What did he want?'

'I think he was planning to seduce me. He's used to getting his way with women. It's funny, no?'

'I'm not laughing.'

•

The next morning Gould and Rose dropped Élodie off at St Pancras and then headed home via the M40 and Oxford. The day was humid and breezy, and Oxford's old chestnuts were releasing their catkins, filling the air with drifts of sweet-smelling pollen. They drove through an archway into New College and were halted by a porter, a young man in a sharp blue suit and university tie. He walked ahead of the car and showed them where to park.

'Thank you, gentlemen,' the porter said as the two detectives climbed from the car. 'I believe you're here to see Professor Fiennes?'

'That's right,' Gould said. 'And Camille Roche, if she's here.'

'Miss Roche has gone down for the vacation I'm afraid. By the way, her name's pronounced Kameeyeh or Kamee. She's French.'

'Thanks for pointing that out to me.'

He ignored the sarcasm: 'My pleasure. If you'd like to follow me back to the lodge, I'll ring the professor.'

'How would you describe Miss Roche?'

'I couldn't say, sir.'

'You don't know her?'

He smiled. 'I didn't say that.'

They had entered the lodge. He took them through to a back office and pointed at a wall chart of passport photographs. 'That's her.'

'You have a photograph of every student?' Rose said.

'It's important that we remember everyone and use their surnames. There are four of us, and the youngest is not too bright.'

'Which one are you?'

'Number two.'

Gould looked at the photograph. A pretty face, like many of the others. Hair tied back; blue eyes; lips parted rather than smiling.

The porter had made his phone call. 'I'll take you to the professor now.'

They walked through a gap in the old town wall and out into the main quad beside the chapel. A sprinkler shot high arcs of water over the oval-shaped lawn.

Gould hadn't yet given up on the porter. 'Does Miss Roche's

sister visit her at all?'

'No.'

'You'd know?'

'Absolutely.'

They heard a window opening and looked up to see an elderly face. 'Come on up.'

The professor wasn't particularly old, but particularly thin and bony, like the bust of Voltaire that stood on his mantelpiece. The booklined room overlooked the college gardens.

'I don't have a kettle but we could go to the SCR if you'd like something?'

'No, we're fine. We need to get back on the road as soon as possible.'

'You're based in York?'

'Yes.'

'Where did you study?'

'Here.'

'College?'

'St Peter's.'

'Umm. Subject?'

'Music.'

'Interesting. Did our paths cross?'

'No.'

He pointed at a settee. 'Let's get down to business.'

'We were hoping to see Camille Roche.'

'She's not here.'

'You're her tutor?'

'Yes. I had a word with Camille before she went down and she told me that she hadn't seen Laura for some time. Charles is concerned, of course, but believes the girl has simply run away. He wouldn't have involved the police at this stage. It was his wife, Laura's mother, who made the call.'

'So, you know the family well?'

'Yes. Charles and I are old friends. It's reasonable for you to assume that the two girls confide in each other, and that Camille knows where Laura is, but, for understandable reasons, they've never been close.'

'Understandable reasons?'

'They're not sisters. They're the offspring of Charles and Elisabeth's previous marriages. Camille is Charles's daughter; Laura is Elisabeth's daughter.'

'I didn't know that.'

'The girls were young children when Charles and Elisabeth married. Charles's first wife had died a few years before, so the union wasn't traumatic for Camille; but Charles stole Elisabeth from Laura's father, so there was considerable trauma for her, exacerbated by his death in a car accident.'

'That's very useful information.'

'Don't you chaps do your homework?'

Gould smiled. 'I still need to talk to Camille. It seems to me that barriers are being put up.'

'I doubt it's that. She deserves her holiday.'

'I'd appreciate it if you'd contact Camille and ask her to ring me. A few words over the phone are all I require.'

'I'll see what I can do.'

As the professor was walking Gould and Rose back to the car he said, 'Camille's a good girl.'

'And Laura isn't?'

'I didn't say that.'

4

It was midnight when Gould arrived at the commissariat de police in the sixth arrondissement. There were grills over the lower windows, and a police sign, but otherwise the building looked no different from the adjoining houses in the rue de l'Abbaye: the higher floors had the same white shutters and elegant window frames. Opposite, a small garden nestled beneath the high walls of the church of Saint-Germain-des-Près.

Élodie met Gould in the vestibule and led him up the stairs. She was wearing jeans and a tight T-shirt. A handgun in a holster, attached to her leather belt, rested against her right hip. It seemed too big for her small frame. 'I'm glad you were able to come over. When we found out that Brenton was in Paris at a summit it seemed like a good opportunity to catch him off guard. Laura's phone records show that he was calling her after she left his employ.' They entered an office where two young men, also wearing jeans and guns, were waiting. 'This is my colleague Marcel, from Bordeaux, and Pierre of the Paris police.'

Gould felt a little awkward in his suit. 'Do you have him yet?'

'You missed the fun at the hotel,' Marcel said in French.

'He was with his secretary,' Élodie said. 'The woman with the ponytail. She's here too. They're in separate rooms.'

'Has he asked for his lawyer?'

'No.'

'I don't like him,' Pierre said. 'We're keeping him waiting. Have you eaten?'

'No.'

'Let's go and eat. We can deal with the suspect later. If Élodie agrees?'

'It's your show,' Élodie said.

'There's a good Lebanese restaurant near here that will be open. Okay?'

It was gone two when they returned to the station. Brenton was sitting calmly at the side of a table in a basement interrogation room. He merely shook his head when he saw Gould enter the room with Marcel, Pierre and Élodie. Marcel and Élodie sat together at the table; Gould leant against a wall.

'You know Inspector Gould, I think?' Marcel said in English.

'Yes.'

'He's here as an observer.'

'Fine. I hope he doesn't pick up any bad habits.'

Pierre had moved behind Brenton's chair. He kicked it away

and Brenton crashed to the floor.

Marcel said, 'What are you doing on the floor? Please sit opposite us in the correct manner.'

Brenton did so, but with the pretend nonchalance of a violent man who knows he is outnumbered. Pierre squeezed his shoulder. Brenton looked him the eyes and said, 'I like your style.'

'He doesn't speak English. Are you sure about the lawyer?'

'For now. I can cope with your games.'

'You'd rather continue to keep your relationship with your secretary hidden, is that not the case?'

'Yes, of course, but not desperately.'

'You're not worried it will damage your career?'

'No. I'm not a politician. I'm not even a civil servant. It's not illegal to have an affair with your secretary.'

'And your nanny, did you treat her that way too?'

'At last we get to it.'

'You were having a sexual relationship with Laura Roche?'

'Yes. She was working for me and living in my house. Droit du seigneur.'

'You really are a charming person, Mr Brenton.'

'Why didn't you tell us the truth in London?' Élodie asked.

'I thought it was implied. It's not relevant.'

'Not relevant? We know you were trying to talk to her after she left London.'

'I rang her mobile a few times.'

'Why did you ring her?'

'I wanted to see her.'

'Laura ended the relationship, not you?'

'Yes and no. She ended it and said she was leaving but we met a few more times for sex. I then decided not to see her again. That's all.'

'When did you last see her?'

'Late May. I don't remember the exact date.'

'Where did you meet?'

'At my cottage near York.'

'For absolute clarity, Mr Brenton, is it the truth that you were having a consensual sexual relationship with Laura that ended, and that you have not had any contact with her since the end of May?'

'Yes, that's the truth.'

'You're lying,' Marcel said.

'No.'

'Given that Laura is missing, we must consider other possibilities,' Élodie said. 'That she ended the affair but you wouldn't accept it. Or, that you ended it, and she threatened to tell your wife. Either scenario gives you a motive to harm her.'

'No.'

'Do you know where Laura is?' Marcel said.

'No.'

'Have you killed her?'

'Don't be absurd.'

Élodie whispered something in Marcel's ear and then walked over to Gould. 'Let's question his assistant.'

Gould waited in the corridor while Élodie went to a drinks machine. She came back with an espresso in a small plastic cup.

'If they're going to hit him about I want to watch,' Gould said.

'They're not going to hit him about,' Élodie said.

The woman had been crying. 'What's going on? You can't keep me here like this.'

'You can phone someone if you like.'

'No, Jeremy told me not to.'

Élodie handed her the coffee. 'Your name is Katherine?'

'Yes.'

'We're sorry it's taking so long. We've been talking to Jeremy. Did you know he was having an affair with his au pair, Laura?'

'No.'

'It doesn't surprise you?'

'He has lots of women.'

'Did you know Laura?'

'Not really. I saw her around the house. Please, will you tell me why I've been arrested?'

'You haven't been arrested. You'll be free to go soon.'

Élodie and Gould went back to the other interrogation room. She nodded at Marcel.

'Okay, you can go,' he told Brenton.

The police officers went back upstairs. The windows were open. Below, Brenton and Katherine emerged from the building. 'For God's sake, shut the fuck up,' Brenton snapped. He grabbed her arm and pulled her away in the direction of the Boulevard Saint-

Germain.

'Where are you staying?' Élodie asked Gould.

'A hotel near the Luxembourg.' He looked at his watch. 'But it's hardly worth it. My flight's at nine.'

'You'll get a couple hours of sleep. I'll drive you.'

Élodie said goodbye to her colleagues. Downstairs, she placed the gun in a locker, and removed the leather belt from the hooks in her jeans.

'Give me a moment, Tom.'

With her back to Gould, she pulled the T-shirt over her head and put on a salmon pink blouse.

They went down to the small courtyard. 'I'm embarrassed that I missed the fact that the Roche girls are not sisters,' Élodie said. 'We had no reason to think otherwise. They both use his name, and he's very private about his family.'

'Does it change anything?'

'I don't know. It explains his attitude. His wife called the police.'

'Against his wishes.'

Élodie pointed at one of the powerful scooters and smiled.

'I can just about handle it.'

'Okay…'

She handed him a helmet. 'You don't trust me?'

He climbed on behind her. She started the machine and manoeuvred it out of the narrow gateway. They drove around the church and onto the wide boulevard. It was deserted of traffic. Ahead, along the whole straight distance of the road, beneath the trees and between the rows of closed shops and restaurants, they could see traffic lights changing from red to green and back to red again. Their helmets tapped. The wind parted and lifted her blouse to reveal the small of her back. At the hotel, in the narrow rue de l'Odéon, she took off the helmet and waited for him to speak; but he hesitated. She stretched forward and kissed him on each cheek, and, within moments, was gone.

5

Karen placed a cup of tea on the table in front of Raymond Pariselle and sat down opposite him.

Élodie didn't recognize Pariselle at first. His hair was uncombed, and his everyday clothes were ill-fitting and worn. She had just arrived after a week's absence, and Brown had taken her straight to the viewing room. 'I don't understand. Why is he here?'

'We did a background check. He was arrested on suspicion of a sex offence back in France.'

'When?'

'Late 1970s. It explains why he left the country.'

'I worked for him for a year. There were lots of girls there. His conduct was harmless.'

'Perhaps you were too old for him. He was accused of molesting a minor.'

'Laura isn't a child, if that's where you're going.'

'Are you saying I should ignore it?'

'No.'

'Would you like to go in there?'

'No, it would humiliate him.'

'I've given this to Karen to try to make it less intimidating for him.'

'Better a man, surely, than a young woman?'

'If you didn't know him would you care?'

'I'm suggesting that a man will get more out of him.'

'Karen did the work and the others are busy. Do you want me to do it?'

'No, of course not. You'd scare him to death.'

Karen was going through the formalities. 'This is just routine, Mr Pariselle, relating to the disappearance of Laura Roche that we've already spoken to you about. As part of an investigation like this it's normal to check criminal records and we know about your arrest some years ago in France and would like to ask you some questions relating to it.'

'You've made a mistake.'

'I don't think so.'

'It was a lifetime ago, in another country. It has no bearing on my life here and I won't talk about it.'

'I'm sure we can clear this up, Mr Pariselle, if you cooperate.'

'I wasn't convicted of any crime. I was the victim... it ruined my life. No one can know. If people know I'll have to leave, and I'm too old.'

'It won't take long.'

'I want to go home. I won't answer your questions. I can't breathe in here.'

He rose awkwardly and clutched the table to steady his balance.

'Are you okay? Should I call a doctor?'

'No, please just let me leave...'

'Please sit down, Mr Pariselle.'

'No. Charge me or I leave.'

'Please wait here.'

Karen joined Brown and Élodie in the viewing room. 'I think he might collapse, sir.'

Brown nodded. 'Okay, we'll leave it for now.'

Upstairs in the incident room Élodie went over to Karen. 'Was it really necessary to bring him in?'

'It was DI Gould's decision.'

'Who did you contact in France?'

'I'll email you the details. Tom spoke to someone on the phone.'

'Things get lost in translation.'

'I didn't enjoy doing that interview.'

Élodie nodded. 'We should go for a drink while I'm here. We're the only women in this room after all.'

'Yes... okay.' Karen was sitting in front of two computer screens, watching CCTV footage. 'I'm looking at the tapes from York Station, trying to spot Laura.'

For a few minutes they watched the black and white images together. One screen showed the concourse; the other the street outside. Karen rewound the file. 'There's one good possibility…'

Élodie looked closely at the shots of a woman crossing the concourse. She shrugged. 'It's hard to know.'

'I've also been looking at couples since she could have met someone on the train and that would give us a line of inquiry. Once I've assembled all the possibilities I'll get the tech guys to see if they can enhance the images.'

'You're right to look at these tapes,' Élodie said. 'It would be helpful to verify that she arrived back in York as the evidence suggests. We know she bought a ticket. What else?'

'We know she told her boss at the café that she was back in York.'

'But she could have been lying.'

Karen nodded. 'Her neighbours haven't been able to help. We haven't found anyone who saw her on the day of her return or subsequently. I'll keep working on this.'

•

That evening Élodie went to Pariselle's restaurant. The maître d' told her that he was worried because the patron hadn't come back. 'I've never known him to miss a service. He's not answering his phone.'

Pariselle lived in an old three storey house further along the quay. The blinds were drawn. Élodie looked up at the dark windows and rang Karen. 'When did we let Pariselle go?'

'A few hours ago. He was driven to his home.'

She walked down the narrow path at the side of the building and into the walled garden at the rear. The enclosed space was laid out with pathways and bay trees in boxes in the French manner. The back door was unlocked. A cat appeared from nowhere and squeezed ahead of her into the house. The kitchen, all shining chrome and copper pots, was spotlessly clean. She called out Pariselle's name as she explored the house, turning on the lights to reveal rooms opulently decorated with antique furniture and statuettes. Was it experience or instinct that made her fear the worse? She climbed the stairs.

One of the bedroom doors was open. She could hear a creaking noise. A shadow moved like a pendulum against the wall. For a few seconds Élodie stood still on the landing, waiting for the courage to enter the room. Pariselle was hanging from a beam by a leather belt. She knew that he had been dead for some time but stood on the kicked away chair to check his pulse. An empty bottle of vodka lay on its side on the floorboards. She looked in vain for a note, and then left the house. She sat on the river wall and phoned the station.

•

Élodie was still sitting beside the river when Gould arrived. Crime scene and forensic officers were working in the house. Gould was wary of the hurt and sadness in Élodie's eyes. 'If you're angry with me, I'm sorry,' he said.

'Why didn't you talk to me before pulling him in?'

'Why should I?'

'Because I knew him.'

'Well, you weren't here.'

'What is the point of us if we just create more misery?'

A constable came over. 'You need to see this, sir.'

In the brightly lit basement there were computers, photographic equipment and box files neatly arranged on metal shelves. One of the white walls was covered by hundreds of photographs of young women. There were many pictures of the same few subjects, arranged in named groups. The women had been photographed secretly as they went about their everyday lives, walking in the street, shopping or entering houses, but also in a changing room as they undressed.

'That's the waitresses' room in the restaurant,' Élodie said. 'He had a secret camera.' She pointed at the pictures of Laura. 'There are more of her than anyone else.'

They studied the pictures silently for a while, slowly walking the length of the room, and finally standing side by side before the section devoted to Laura.

'There are pictures of me from ten years ago over there,' Élodie said.

'Yes. He was at this for a long time.' He pointed at one of the photographs. 'This shows Laura entering the Novotel hotel. She was meeting a man, right? We'll be able to get the dates from the originals on his computer.'

Élodie turned to one of the other officers. 'Can you get us the dates of these? And ring us straight away? I expect he organized everything in named folders, so look for Laura.'

'I'll bet there's video too,' Gould said.

'You agree that Raymond Pariselle was not guilty of anything other than being a peeping tom?'

'No, I don't agree at all.'

'Shall we check out the hotel?'

'It can wait until tomorrow.'

'I need to do something.'

'There's still work to be done here.'

'I'll go alone then.'

'You can't do that. I'll phone Karen and tell her to meet you there.'

After she had left Gould went over to the officers who were looking at the photographs of Élodie. 'If anyone has a laugh or gossips about the photos of lieutenant Duquette all hell will break loose. Do I make myself clear?'

•

Karen joined Élodie in the hotel bar.

'Thank you for coming,' Élodie said. 'Tom wouldn't let me do this alone.'

'That's okay.'

'It hasn't ruined your evening?'

'No, I was at home. I'll have a glass.'

Élodie poured Karen a glass of wine.

'Tom phoned with the date, 22 May. I've just spoken to the manager.' She handed Élodie a sheet of paper. 'That's a printout of the register. Whose name are you hoping to find?'

'Jeremy Brenton.'

'His name isn't there. This place is too downmarket for him.'

'It's a good place for a man to take a woman if he wants anonymity.'

Karen took a sip of wine. She watched Élodie's frown turn into a look of puzzlement, almost a smile. 'No, he's not here, but his PA is... Katherine Moore.'

She placed the sheet on the table.

'So Brenton was here but not booked in?'

'Maybe. The CCTV should tell us. It's a lead, anyway.'

'But surely this is a red herring? Raymond Pariselle is our prime suspect?'

'I think we're going to discover that Raymond is the red herring.'

'He could have changed since you knew him.'

'He had changed. He seemed diminished.'

'I'm sorry, it must have been upsetting to find him.'

'When I was eighteen Raymond was kind to me. He had real authority back then.'

Karen smiled awkwardly. 'Should we take some statements and

ask about the CCTV?'

'Yes, you go ahead. I'll join you in a minute.'

•

'So, where are we?' Brown asked. 'Is this now a murder case?'

'Traces of Laura's DNA have been found in Raymond Pariselle's house,' Gould said.

'Blood?'

'No.'

'His car?'

'We can't find it. It's not parked in any of the streets near the house. We've checked all the rented garages and car parks in the area. We've put out a call, but nothing yet.'

'What about the neighbours?'

'Nothing, sir,' Rose said. 'It seems he was a loner. His neighbours can't remember seeing anyone else entering the property.'

'I think he was a voyeur, nothing more,' Élodie said.

'He was a voyeur on an industrial scale,' Gould said. 'The evidence suggests that his behaviour would have escalated to something more than just taking pictures. Why was Laura in his house?'

'She worked for him, why shouldn't she have gone to his home?'

'Did you, when you worked for him?'

'Yes. He lived in a flat above the restaurant then.'

'Okay, what else?' Brown said.

'We found a number of keys we can't account for in his house,' Gould said. 'I think he had one or more lockups, and possibly other properties. If the lockups are in York it shouldn't be long before we find them.'

'Are you going to bring in Brenton's PA Katherine Moore?' Élodie asked.

'No, I want everyone to concentrate on Pariselle,' Brown said. 'He may have locked Laura up somewhere.'

'We are justified in suspecting Brenton and Moore because they have been lying about Laura,' Élodie said. 'We've been through the CCTV footage and Miss Moore arrived and left the hotel alone. Laura arrived at seven thirty and didn't leave until early the next morning. She didn't book a room so I think she stayed in Miss Moore's room.'

'Have you found any evidence that Brenton was at the hotel that night?'

'No, none.'

'The evidence against Brenton isn't strong enough.'

'He's lying for a reason,' Karen said. 'His PA met Laura that night for a reason.'

'It could have been a coincidence,' Rose said. 'Laura could have been meeting any of the men staying at the hotel.'

'I don't think so,' Élodie said.

'It's a legitimate line of enquiry,' Brown said. 'I want to park it for now. Who's working on tracing the other girls in the photographs?'

'I am, sir,' Karen said.

'I want to know who they are and where they are by the end of the day.'

'Who they are is easy. He was very methodical in naming them on his computer. I've crosschecked with the restaurant's personnel records. They were all waitresses. So far we've accounted for half of them.'

'Alive and well?'

'Yes. I'm also trying to work out the locations of the pictures that show Laura. There are a couple of pictures that show her entering the staff door of a lap dancing club in Leeds.'

'Jesus,' Rose mumbled. 'Quelle fille.'

'What does that mean?' Brown asked.

'Nothing, sir.'

'No, please, share your wisdom with the group.'

'This Laura is quite a girl. No disrespect to lieutenant Duquette. We're all thinking it.'

'Thank you for sharing. I don't know what we'd do without your insights.'

Everyone laughed except for Élodie and Karen.

'Happy to help, sir,' Rose said.

'Anything else? Right, get on with it then. All leave cancelled.'

Brown gestured to Élodie and Gould that they should follow him into his office. He told them to sit down on the old leather couch that took up most of the space in the glass sided room.

'I've had Brenton's political masters, and the Chief Super,

telling me to leave him alone. Believe me, as a consequence there's nothing I'd like more than to arrest him. He's hiding behind his lawyer, so we'll need a strong reason to interview him again. Okay, he's been lying repeatedly about Laura, but he doesn't want his wife or superiors, or for that matter the girl's father, to know about the affair. His wife, by the way, has a mental illness. I have a letter from her doctor. Given her condition I can well believe that Brenton would lie about Laura. As for his secretary, it's intriguing but explicable. Two women who worked for the same man and knew each other. Perhaps they were friends.'

'I accept that you need to put all your resources into investigating Raymond Pariselle,' Élodie said.

'Is Charles Roche in the UK at the moment?'

'No, he's in Bordeaux. I have to fly back today.'

•

Élodie caught a train to London. From King's Cross she walked the short distance over the railroad tracks to Somers Town. The grey green sky was weighed down by a storm that never broke; the heat was humid and sticky. Rows of old houses of yellow brick were in places separated by newer buildings, schools and community centres erected in the 1950s and 60s in the gaps made by German bombs. With her trained eye she noticed the surveillance cameras at the end of every street and the 'no loitering' signs. She turned a corner, and walked by a playground where a girl, sitting

'No. Listen…' She paused to light a cigarette. 'Laura is a troubled girl. She's reckless. She seemed to be always on the run, if that makes sense. You'll do your best?'

'My best?'

'To find her. To bring her back safely from whatever dark place has claimed her.'

'Yes, I promise.'

'Does her family care about her?'

'Why do you ask that?'

'She seemed to hate her parents. She said they didn't care about her. But then, she lied about everything.'

They were silent for a moment.

'Thank you for your honesty, Katherine.'

'Kate, or Kathy, not Katherine. Can we sit here for a moment longer?'

'Yes. I like it here.'

'I come here when I want to find some peace. Over there Mary Wollstonecraft is buried. She died giving birth to a daughter, Mary. When Mary was a girl she gave her virginity to Shelley at her mother's grave.'

'Is that true?'

'I don't know.'

They walked back to Kate's building. 'Would you like to come up?'

'I have a flight to catch. But thank you.'

'No problem. Maybe next time.'

PART TWO

6

Élodie's flight landed at Bordeaux airport shortly before midnight. As she exited the terminal she saw her boss leaning against his car.

'This is good of you.'

'We need to talk.'

Capitaine Bercot was wearing his habitual black suit. Tall and thin, with knowing eyes behind round spectacles, he looked more like a clergyman than a policeman. The journey started in silence. Bercot wasn't one for small talk. Élodie couldn't remember having an exchange of words with him that was not related to work. She respected him. She waited for him to speak.

The outer suburbs of retail parks and motels were sliced in two by the straight road. Bercot drove at speed with one hand on the steering wheel. Soon they were on the old treelined avenue that led to the centre. He turned to look at her for a few seconds.

'Capitaine Brown thinks that Mlle Roche is dead, and that he has her murderer,' Bercot said. 'Is he right?'

'He's right to pursue it.'

'But you have doubts?'

'Yes, but my opinion is compromised. As I said on the phone, I knew the suspect.'

'Could Mlle Roche be alive, tied up somewhere?'

'Capitaine Brown and his team are working on that basis, but no one believes it.'

'I've updated Charles Roche. He's asked for a first-hand report from you. Brown wants to go public and will. Roche's agreement isn't needed but ask for his permission anyway.'

Bercot was manoeuvring the car down the narrow streets of the Chartrons quarter.

'Listen, Élodie, if I'd known you were familiar with York and were going to end up knowing the prime suspect I would never have sent you. And what are you up to with Roche?'

'What do you mean?'

'He thinks you're cold and disinterested. It wouldn't hurt you to be friendlier.'

'He doesn't respect me as a police officer. When he looks at me he sees a girl.'

'I don't care. He plays golf with the Commissaire.'

'So you keep telling me.'

They had reached Élodie's home in the rue Notre Dame. She swung her legs out of the car and turned to thank him, but the car was already speeding away in the narrow space between the bollards. She went into the bar across the street and ordered an espresso. She exchanged a few words with the bar staff and then sat at a table on the pavement. She looked up at the little balcony and the dark windows of her apartment. It was only when the bar closed that she went home.

•

Élodie decided to dress casually in a T-shirt and linen trousers. She walked down the street to where her pale blue Renault Clio was parked.

She drove out of Bordeaux and took the estuary road. Soon the car was surrounded by a flat patchwork of vineyards. Copses and white stone buildings occasionally broke the monotony of land and sky. Through the open windows, as the breeze brushed against her face, Élodie could sense the imposing presence of the Gironde in the fishy odour of muddy water; sometimes, to her right, the estuary could be seen for a fleeting moment.

She came to a village and realised that she had driven passed the entrance to Roche's estate. She was expecting a grand architectural statement. Driving back down the road she saw on her left a simple stone gateway. A white track, ruler straight, cut through the vines towards the estuary. For a moment she felt she had gone back in time. People were working in the fields, bent over like Millet's peasants, their faces shaded by straw hats; horses were pulling carts and machinery. However, a little further on she passed a hi-tech building of glass and steel. She came to a turning, a driveway guarded by tall plane trees that led to the château.

The château was an old building of precise symmetries. The white shutters merged with the stonework and the steep grey mansard roof gave the structure a stately elegance. The house was as beautiful as the black Jaguar E Type and the silver Mercedes SLS that were parked either side of the entrance steps. Élodie parked her dented and dirty Renault beside the gleaming Mercedes.

A young man in a suit walked down the steps to greet her. 'Lieutenant Duquette? Monsieur Roche is working in the vineyard. He asked me to take you.'

He led her to where more vehicles were parked beneath the trees at the side of the house.

'Is it far?'

'Not far.'

'Do you mind if I walk?'

He looked puzzled. 'If you're sure? I'll show you the way.'

They walked on through the trees to the open country. The young man pointed towards the Gironde. 'You'll find Monsieur Roche down there, near the water.'

Élodie thanked him and followed the gravelled path beside the vines. The land sloped gently and the estuary was spread out like an immense spillage of liquid mud. To her right she noticed a helipad. The estate workers were predominantly young – teenage boys and girls wearing khaki shorts and T-shirts stamped with a discreet 'Château Roche' logo. They tended the vines with the care of conservators handling ancient artefacts.

As Élodie neared the water's edge she heard an engine and turned to see a man riding a motorbike along the dirt track that marked the end of the vineyard, trailing a plume of clay coloured dust. The man wore white trousers and a loose green shirt that billowed around his hips. He wore sunglasses but no helmet. At a distance he looked like Steve McQueen in The Great Escape. It was only as the bike neared that Élodie realised that the rider was Roche. He braked to a halt, dismounted and held out his hand for Élodie to shake. This informal and courteous version of Roche was disconcerting.

'We can talk in here,' Roche said.

A wooden fishing hut, a carrelet, rose from the water on stilts. Élodie followed Roche across the narrow wooden bridge and onto the platform. Instead of fishing gear the hut housed expensive furniture, modern gadgets, a coffee machine and a minibar. It was like a room in a luxury hotel. The hut was surrounded by the milky brown water.

'You see?' Roche said. 'Things are often not what they seem. We should live our lives on that basis. Please sit down. What would you like to drink?'

'Coffee, please.'

Roche worked the machine. He handed her the cup and sat in the chair beside her.

'I was surprised to see horses,' Élodie said.

'Yes. In recent years we've examined everything. The

reintroduction of horses has been a major part of that. It is about respecting the soil as well as lowering our carbon footprint. Similarly, we care for the environment by only using organic methods to fight insects and disease. As for the winemaking, everything is state-of-the-art. We're not as grand or as prestigious as Latour or our other neighbours, but our wine has been consistently good in recent years.'

'I was stung by your criticism of my ignorance of our region's wine production,' Élodie lied. 'I've been reading up. I know, for instance, that the Gironde estuary produces fine wines because of the particular nature of the climate and the soil, the presence of gravel and clay.'

'Simplistic but true,' Roche said.

'I know also that your family have been making wine here since the 18th century.'

'My forbears grew rich, as did many of their contemporaries, exporting wine to England and Holland. It is the trade I'm still in. But people were making wine here much earlier. During the Hundred Years War this place belonged to the English.' With hardly a pause Roche changed the subject. 'Bercot told me about the restaurateur. Have you anything to add?'

'Capitaine Brown wants to go public. Can I tell him that you agree?'

'We won't be attending a press conference, but, yes, I agree.'

'Can I ask you something?'

'Of course.'

'I don't understand how you can be so calm. About Laura.'

'I'm not calm. Hiding feelings that reveal vulnerability is something they beat into me at boarding school.' He was silent for a moment. 'The only way to cope is to keep busy. I want to show you something.'

Roche took Élodie to a hanger near the helipad. Inside, there were a number of boats including, at the far end, a canoe hanging from the ceiling beams. 'This is a cockleshell canoe,' Roche said. 'Have you heard of Operation Frankton?'

'Yes, of course, it was a British raid to destroy German cargo ships docked in Bordeaux.'

'This is one of the canoes used by the commandos. They had to paddle from the mouth of the estuary all the way to Bordeaux, a journey of some ninety miles, navigating the tidal current and evading the German navy. Rough weather at the mouth of the Gironde did for four of the soldiers. Four of the others were captured by local gendarmes while resting onshore and handed over to the Germans. Only two canoes, four men, reached the docks. They placed limpet mines on six vessels and escaped undetected back downstream. They landed not far from here. My father gave the four men shelter on the estate for nearly three weeks while an escape route was planned. Two made it home. Of the twelve men who started the mission, six were executed by the Germans.'

They walked through the vines. Roche stopped to talk to members of his staff and to appreciate their work. He placed his hand on the small of Élodie's back to allow her to walk ahead of him down one of the narrow channels. She risked a question. 'Is Camille here?'

He was close behind her. 'No.'

They had reached the avenue of trees.

'I know that my treatment of you has been somewhat ungracious. I've tried to make amends today. Is that true?'

'Yes.'

'Do you acknowledge that I'm being sincere?'

'Yes.'

'Good.' He looked at his watch. 'I have to go now.'

Élodie was taken aback. 'Is that all?'

'For now.' As he walked back into the vineyard he called, 'I've left some bottles for you.'

Élodie returned to her car. The young man appeared carrying a crate of wine. He placed it in the boot of her car. 'Monsieur Roche also wanted you to have this.' He handed her a T-shirt.

•

Élodie looked in the rear-view mirror and saw that the Jaguar convertible was drawing close. She moved over onto the verge beside the vines. As the Jag came level she saw that the driver was Elisabeth Roche. 'Please follow me,' Elisabeth Roche said.

The Jag took a right turn, close to the boundary wall of the estate. The track led to a small house. A canopy of foliage shaded a terrace, and to the right there was a swimming pool. Élodie parked beside the Jag and joined Elisabeth on the terrace. They shook hands. Elisabeth unlocked the door and they entered the kitchen. 'We can talk here,' she said, indicating the table. 'Would you like something?'

'No, I'm fine thank you.'

'Well, I need a drink.' She opened a cupboard and took out a bottle of Cognac. She returned to the table and poured herself a glass. 'My husband didn't want me to speak with you. He thinks I need protecting. Please don't tell him.'

'Of course not.'

'I'm terrified for my daughter.'

'We're doing everything we can, Madame Roche.'

'This man who was stalking her… Do you think he's harmed her? Do you think my girl is dead?'

'There are still other possibilities. Can you tell me anything about Laura that might help?'

'She doesn't confide in me. I've brought you here because this is where Laura lives when she's home. If you go through her things you might find something that I've missed.'

She took Élodie upstairs. 'The room at the end is Laura's.'

'Does Camille sleep here too?'

'Yes, when she's home. The girls both stay here, but rarely at the same time. I'll wait in the kitchen.'

There were no personal items in Laura's bedroom, other than some toiletries on the dressing table and a few items of clothing. Élodie took out each drawer and removed the clothes. She searched the pockets. She looked behind the wardrobe and under the bed. She lifted the mattress.

Next she went into Camille's room. It looked little lived-in too, but at least there were some books and CDs. Élodie was disappointed not to find a computer or diary. The only item of interest was a large photo album. Flipping through the pages Élodie saw that the album covered the period from Camille and Laura's childhood to the near present.

She carried the album down to the kitchen. 'Only this is of possible interest.'

'Where did you find it?'

'In Camille's room.'

'I didn't say you could go in there.'

'Can I take it with me?'

'No. Camille will notice it's gone and then Charles will know that I've gone behind his back.'

'Are you expecting Camille?'

'No.'

'I just need it for a few days to make some copies, then I'll return it. It may be of value.'

'All right, but please be discreet.'

'How would you describe your husband's relationship with Laura?'

'What do you mean?'

'She isn't his child.'

'He brought her up as his own. He loves her.'

Instead of returning to Bordeaux, Élodie drove across the Médoc into a countryside of sand and pines. With the sea on her right, she followed a private lane that led to a small beach house. She walked through the garden – a fenced off area of the dune, with clumps of grass and herbs growing out of the sand – and onto the wooden boards of the terrace. She found the key beneath a flowerpot.

There was a message from her mother on the table. 'There's a bottle of wine in the fridge, darling. Will we see you on your birthday?'

She poured herself a glass of the white wine and phoned her mother. There was no reply. She sent a text to Gould: 'Please call me.'

Her phone bleeped almost immediately.

'Is everything okay?' Gould asked.

'Yes. Why don't you come over for the weekend?'

'Yes, I'd like that.'

•

At police headquarters, in rue François de Sourdis, Marcel joined Élodie in one of the conference rooms. The snapshots in Camille's album had been scanned onto a computer connected to an overhead projector. Élodie was viewing each one on a screen in the darkened room.

'Anything?' Marcel asked.

She shook her head. 'Lots of pictures of Camille with girls and boys her own age. 'I've only identified Laura in one picture.'

She pressed a key. The picture showed Camille and Laura sitting together in a summer garden, smiling, their arms draped around each other.

'It's only surprising because I'd come to the conclusion that the girls are not close.'

'We're wasting our time on this,' Marcel said. 'If she came from an ordinary family would we be doing anything? These wine aristos think they own Bordeaux.'

'Charles Roche gave me a crate of wine yesterday,' Élodie said.

'How many bottles?'

'Twelve. He probably does the same for all his visitors.'

'I don't think so. His wine sells for hundreds of Euros a bottle. So that means he's given you thousands of Euros.'

'I didn't realise.'

'You have to give it back.'

She opened the blinds. There were patches of blue sky, but a curtain of rain drifted in the sunlight. The twin spires of the cathedral pricked a grey cloud. In the car park, far below, a silver Mercedes was circling. 'Talk of the devil,' she whispered.

'Perhaps we should leave this to the English?'

'Perhaps.'

'We have other priorities.'

'I'll work on this in my spare time.'

'At least until there's something we can get our teeth into.'

'Okay, I agree.'

'Where did you disappear to that night in Paris? With the English detective.'

'Why do you care? How are your wife and kids?'

'I'm just concerned. You're away most of the time and when you're here you seem distracted. You didn't come into work after visiting Roche.'

'I went to the beach.'

'You went to the beach?'

'Yes.'

'What's wrong with you, Élodie?'

A young woman entered the room. 'Charles Roche is here. He's asked to see you.'

'Let me deal with him,' Marcel said.

'No.'

Élodie went into the washroom and checked her hair and makeup before going down to the reception hall. Roche greeted her with formal courtesy. 'Are you free?'

'Yes, but I only have an hour.'

'Just an aperitif at the Grand Hotel. My daughter will join us.'

'Camille?'

'Yes. Are you pleased?'

'Yes, of course.'

'She wants her album back. Do you have it?'

'Yes.' Élodie paused. 'Your wife was only trying to help.'

'Don't worry, Mademoiselle, I'm not cross with my wife.'

Élodie went to fetch the album. 'Charles Roche is finally letting me interview his daughter,' she told Marcel. 'I think we should set up surveillance.'

'Why?'

'Because he's not going to let me talk to her alone and I want to see where she goes and who she meets.'

'I don't think it's justified.'

'Just one person to follow the girl. We're meeting at the Grand Hotel. Will you set it up?'

'No, I don't agree.'

Élodie joined Roche in the lobby. The storm had yet to pass over. Roche shielded Élodie with his umbrella and opened the car door for her. He drove to the place de la Comédie and pulled up outside the hotel. A concierge took charge of the car and the maître d' showed them to one of the best tables on the terrace. Roche asked the maître d' after his family and listened patiently. He ordered a bottle of wine.

'From your estate?' Élodie asked.

'No. A Pessac white. Here she is.'

He was looking in the direction of the opera house. For a few seconds a tram blocked the view. Its passing revealed a girl walking across the square in the light rain, her head down, as if lost in a reverie. Roche called out to her.

'Will you let me talk to Camille alone?'

'I'm going to say no, but only because she's not coping very well with Laura's disappearance. Don't tell her about the restaurant owner. I don't want her to worry. I'll tell her myself when I think she's ready.'

Camille had reached the terrace. She smiled at her father. He kissed her and held her hand for a moment. 'This is lieutenant Duquette.'

Camille sat in the chair beside Élodie. A pair of sunglasses held back her fair hair. Her complexion was pale and lightly freckled; her brown eyes belonged in a different face. She was nervous. She played with her bracelets, and yawned.

'The album's in my car,' Roche told her. 'Sometimes the police have to be intrusive.'

'It's fine,' she said, but her tone suggested otherwise.

Élodie gave Camille her card. 'In case you ever want to call me.'

A waiter arrived with the wine. Another brought a plate of hors d'oeuvre.

'Camille is on her way to the Midi,' Roche said. 'Then she returns to Oxford. Soon she'll be Dr Roche.'

She turned her head to look at her father and left a pause before saying, in English, 'Dad, please.'

'What's the subject of your doctorate?' Élodie asked.

Camille left another pause. 'Is that relevant?'

Roche frowned. 'It could be relevant or it could be polite conversation. I think probably the latter. Please be polite, Camille.'

'Broadly speaking, it's about letter writing as a means of intellectual exchange in the 18th century.'

Élodie nodded. 'So you've lived in Oxford for a number of

years?'

'Yes, it's my home now. Shouldn't we talk about Laura? That's why I'm here.'

Élodie reached into her bag and took out an envelope. 'We've been looking at the surveillance footage taken at York station on the day Laura returned to York, just so that we can verify that she did return to the city.' She placed a large black and white photograph in front of Camille and Roche. 'Is this Laura?'

'Why is the image quality always so poor?' Roche asked.

'It's expensive to upgrade thousands of cameras with digital.'

'It's her,' Camille said.

'Are you sure? She's wearing sunglasses.'

'I'm sure. I know my sister's face and hair, and the ankle boots and handbag are hers.'

'Not many girls own a Louis Vuitton handbag, lieutenant,' Roche said.

'Thank you for confirming.'

'Were you able to find her on other cameras?' Roche asked.

'There's a camera in the street outside the station, but after that we lose her.'

Camille placed the photograph face down on the table. 'It's creepy seeing her like this.'

'Do you know where Laura is?'

'Of course I don't know where she is. I would have said. Why would I lie?'

'Because of a promise between sisters.'

She shook her head. 'No.'

'When did you last see her?'

'Back in the spring.'

'In France?'

'Here.'

'She came home for my birthday,' Roche said.

'Did she say anything to you about her life in England? About the people she was seeing?'

'Nothing.'

'And you didn't get together in England?'

'We met once in Oxford when she first came over. It may seem odd to you, but we didn't get on. It doesn't mean I didn't love her…'

Camille started to cry. Roche put his arm around her shoulders. She rested her head against his chest. She was sobbing uncontrollably.

'I'm sorry,' Élodie said.

'Now perhaps you'll understand why I delayed this moment.'

'Should I leave you alone?'

'No, it will pass.'

Camille tried to break free from Roche's embrace, her arms flailing violently. 'It will never pass; it will never pass!'

'Calm down.'

'Let me go!'

Roche released his grip. Camille stumbled between the tables and away from the terrace. She crossed the square and sat on the

Opera house steps. Roche watched her.

After a while he said, absentmindedly, 'Can I give you a lift back?'

'No, thank you, I'll walk.'

Élodie left the restaurant. Before turning the corner she glanced back. It seemed to her that Roche and his daughter were still looking at each other across the wide distance of the square.

7

'There it is,' Rose said as he turned the car off the dual carriageway. The squat redbrick building was the only surviving structure in an area of vacant lots and wasteland. 'It looks more inviting at night.'

'Come here a lot, do you?' Karen said.

He left a pause. 'When I was working for vice in Leeds. Prostitution, dogging, drugtaking and joyriding are the main activities around here at night. We were called out quite often.'

The car park was almost empty. Rose slotted the car between a white Range Rover and a red 911. Inside the club they found a barman cleaning tables.

'I'll get the manager,' he said.

Karen and Rose sat down together at a table near to the circular stage. A smiling middle-aged man in a light grey suit appeared through the red velvet drapes and took hold of the metal pole before jumping off the stage.

'I'm Len,' he said. 'I'm in charge here. Would you prefer to go up to my office?'

'No, here is fine,' Rose said. 'What's your full name?'

'Len Salmon.'

Salmon sat down opposite the detectives.

'Who owns the club these days?'

'We're a legitimate business. The licences are in order, and we take our responsibilities as an employer very seriously.'

'Good for you, but who's the owner?'

'An American company. So, what's the problem? I apply the rules rigidly. There's no prostitution or drugtaking here. I used to be a human rights lawyer.'

Karen took out her iPad and placed it on the table in front of Salmon. 'Do you recognise this girl?'

'She's vaguely familiar. Who is she? All the girls are eighteen or over, if that's what this is about.'

'She's called Laura Roche.'

'No, it doesn't ring a bell.'

'There was a police press conference about her earlier in the week.'

'Didn't see it. Sorry.'

'Why are you lying?' Rose asked. 'She was photographed entering this club. In May of this year.'

'Hundreds of people come to the club every night. We don't keep track of the punters.'

'She was photographed entering by the stage door,' Karen said.

‘What do you want me to say? We have a high turnover.’

Karen told Salmon, ‘I’ll arrest you for obstruction.’

‘I don’t know her. That’s the truth.’

Salmon waved at a woman who had entered the room from a staff door behind the bar. She wore a red cardigan over a stylish green dress. Her dilated pupils suggested a recent hit of cocaine or heroin.

‘This is Megan, one of my assistant managers. Megan looks after the girls.’

‘What’s going on?’ Megan asked.

Salmon handed her the iPad. ‘They think this girl worked here but I can’t recall her.’

Megan pulled up a chair. ‘Yes, I remember her. She worked behind the bar for a short time.’

‘Can you remember her name?’ Karen asked.

Megan shook her head. ‘She was French I think.’

‘She’s called Laura Roche.’

Megan nodded.

‘What do you remember about her?’

‘I remember trying to persuade her to perform. She refused. Which was fine. She wasn’t very good as a waitress. One night she didn’t turn up and that was it. We didn’t see her again.’

‘How did she seem?’

‘What do you mean?’

‘Was she troubled? Did anyone bother her while she was here?’

‘She was just a girl. As I say, she was here for a very short time.’

'And when she didn't turn up, did you try to contact her?'

'I'm sure the duty manager phoned her contact number that night. In a rage no doubt. But… I'm not a fucking social worker.'

'Does it happen a lot? Girls leaving without giving notice?'

'It happens. Not often. I can only think of one other example during the last few months.'

'You're very young,' Rose told Megan.

'Am I?' She touched the hem of her dress. 'I'm older than I look.'

'You're really pretty, but you know that, don't you?'

Karen shot Rose a look. 'We'll need to see your records concerning Laura,' Karen said.

'Fine. It's all on the computer.'

'The other girl who left without notice… Can you tell me about her?'

'A Czech girl called Tereza.'

'Was she a waitress too?'

'No, she was one of our performers.'

'Describe her.'

'Slim. Darkhaired.'

'Did she have any tattoos?'

'All the girls have tattoos.'

'Did she have a small tattoo of a scorpion on her right foot?'

'Yes, I think she did.'

Karen and Rose looked at each other.

'How did you know that?' Megan asked.

'Tell us about Tereza,' Rose said.

'There's nothing to tell. She came looking for work, last winter. She was very sweet, very popular. She said that at the end of a year she planned to go home to go to college. Why are you asking about her?'

'The body of a girl was found in York. We haven't been able to identify her, until now.'

'Tereza? You're sure? How did she die?'

'She drowned in the river.'

'Did someone kill her?'

'No,' Rose said.

Karen frowned. 'Actually, we can't answer that at this stage. Did she know Laura?'

'They were here at the same time, but Laura wasn't around for long enough to make friends with anyone.'

Karen picked up her iPad and displayed a picture of Pariselle. 'Do you recognise this man?'

'No,' Salmon said.

'No,' Megan said.

Karen caressed the screen to display a picture of Brenton. 'What about this man?'

Salmon and Megan exchanged a glance.

'We know him,' Megan said. 'Jeremy Brenton. He comes here quite often. Always with a party of blokes he's entertaining.'

'He spends a lot of cash here,' Salmon said.

'Do you know him personally?' Rose asked.

'I shake his hand and exchange pleasantries when he's in. He's a gold club member, as it were.'

'When was he last here?'

'I don't think we've seen him since the spring.'

'Did Brenton show a particular interest in Tereza?' Karen asked.

'He isn't a difficult customer,' Salmon said. 'He's never pestered a particular girl or done anything questionable.'

'We'll need to interview all your people,' Karen said. 'I'd like you to call everyone in tomorrow morning.'

'Of course, anything you need,' Salmon said.

'They won't all come, not in the morning,' Megan said.

'Anyone who doesn't come will get a visit from us wherever they live. Tell them that.'

'Let me give you my card,' Rose said to Megan.

'We'll leave it there for now,' Karen said.

Rose placed his hand on Karen's shoulder. 'Why don't you have a go before we leave?' He pointed at the pole. 'I'm sure Megan will show you how. Let your hair down.'

When they were out in the car park Karen said, 'What did you say to me? How dare you say that to me in front of them?'

'Get a sense of humour, will you?'

'You think you can talk to a woman like that?'

'I just did. You've turned into such a precious little bitch.'

'Now I'm a bitch?'

'I hate this political correctness shit.'

'I can take a private joke, but you humiliated me in front of the people we were interviewing.'

'So fight back. Slap my face. Give me an excuse to beat you up.'

She stepped back. 'You're out of control.'

'I'm just having a laugh.'

'I don't think you are.'

'You're no fun to work with. Are you jealous of that girl? You know, Karen, you started this with your "Come here a lot?" jibe.'

'That was a harmless joke made in private.'

'Well it put me in a mean mood.'

She walked ahead of him to the car. 'Can I drive?'

'Sure.'

Rose tossed her the keys and walked round to the passenger side. Karen was already in the car. She activated the locks, started the engine and drove off.

•

Karen knocked on Brown's door.

'I know who the girl in the river was,' she said.

Brown joined Karen and Gould in the incident room. She told them about the club.

'Good work,' Brown said. 'Have you arranged to go back to get statements?'

'Yes, tomorrow.'

'Brenton's either guilty of something or he has a knack of being at the wrong place at the right time,' Gould said. 'It's new evidence. We can question him.'

'Yes, fine, but informally. Go to him. And don't get distracted. Find me something conclusive on Pariselle.'

'There's nothing to find. We have his car. Nothing. We've accounted for all the keys. Karen's traced all the girls in the photos. All unharmed; all with fond memories of Pariselle.'

'Something could come out of the appeal.'

'We've had hundreds of calls,' Karen said. 'We're following them up methodically, but nothing significant has jumped out.'

'Let's see what comes out of your investigations at the club tomorrow.'

'When you get to the club tomorrow put the manager and his assistant in a car and bring them here,' Gould said. 'It makes sense to separate them from their staff.'

Brown returned to his office.

'Where's Rose?' Gould said.

'I don't know. I'm not getting on well with him. Can we be separated?'

'What are you talking about?'

'He's sexist, and aggressive. I've had enough.'

'Toughen up. How can I separate you? We work as a team.'

'Fine.'

'Do you want to make a formal complaint?'

'Of course not. I shouldn't have mentioned it. I'm tired, that's all.'

'See if you can get me an appointment with Jeremy Brenton in London on Saturday. I'll break my journey to Bordeaux. Don't insist.'

'Yes, sir.'

Karen went back to her desk. Rose entered the incident room as Gould was leaving. 'Where have you been?' Gould asked.

'I was following something up.'

Rose waited for Gould to leave the room before drawing up a chair behind Karen. His mouth was almost touching her neck.

'Enjoy that, did you? I'll make you pay.'

She continued to type. 'Leave me alone.'

8

'Thank you for coming in,' Gould said to Len Salmon.

'I wasn't aware I had a choice,' Salmon said.

'How long have you been the manager of the club?'

'Two years.'

'Where were you before?'

'In London. I was a lawyer. I expect you're wondering why I – '

'I couldn't care less. Why did you lie when my colleagues asked you about your relationship with Jeremy Brenton?'

'I didn't lie.'

Gould looked down at Karen's report. 'You were asked whether you knew him personally and you said you only exchanged a few words with him when he came to the club.'

'I didn't use the word "only". I was very careful with my words. I said I shook his hand and had a few words; I didn't say that was all I did.'

'I see. You evaded the question.'

'If you like. It doesn't mean I have something to hide. It's my legal training. Old habits die hard. No doubt you've done some digging and discovered that the law firm I worked for in London did work for the Treasury.'

'And that the two of you were contemporaries at Trinity College, Cambridge.'

'Neither fact means that we're co-conspirators.'

'What really goes on when Jeremy Brenton comes to Yorkshire? He doesn't come up here just for a lap dance, does he?'

'Of course not. He has a holiday home up here.'

'If I really start to dig, what am I going to find?'

'Nothing.'

'Did Jeremy Brenton ask you to give Laura Roche a job?'

'No. As I told your colleagues, I can't even remember her. I checked our records: she only worked for us for two weeks, and Jeremy didn't visit the club during those weeks.'

'When did you last see Jeremy?'

'I haven't seen him since May.' Salmon consulted his Blackberry. 'I saw him once in May, on the 18th. Before that… We met once in April, once in February and twice in December.'

'What did you do on the 18th of May?'

'As I recall, he came to the club with friends. We had a drink together at his house in the early hours.'

'Would you like to say anything about Tereza?

'There's nothing to say. She was a good employee. One night

she didn't show.'

'And the other girls? They'll confirm that?'

'I don't know what they'll tell you about Tereza's personal life. But she was properly treated by myself and my team. I don't procure girls for Jeremy Brenton or anyone else, but I can't control what the girls do behind my back in their own time, can I?'

'Would you mind staying for a little bit longer?'

'Sure.'

Gould walked down the corridor and into another interrogation room. Megan was sitting at the table.

'I'm DI Gould.'

Megan nodded.

'Would you like to take off your jacket? It's hot in here.'

Megan slipped out of her jacket and placed it over the back of the chair. Gould took hold of her wrists and stretched her bare arms towards him.

'You look high,' he said. 'Take off your shoes.'

'Fuck you.' For a moment she just stared back at him. Finally she said, 'All right.'

She slipped off her shoes and raised her knees to place her feet on the edge of the chair. He turned away to write a note.

Megan stepped back into her shoes. She pulled her chair up to the table.

'Are you using?'

'No. Why isn't there a policewoman here? Shouldn't there be a woman here?'

'Everything is filmed.' He pointed at the camera. 'Would you like a policewoman to come in and hold your hand?'

'No.'

'What's your job at the club?'

'I'm an assistant manager.'

'How old are you?'

'Twenty.'

'So you're the same age as the girls?'

'Most are eighteen.'

'Were you promoted from the ranks?'

She left a long pause. 'No. Don't you remember me?'

'Of course I remember you.'

'Is that why you're making a fuss about drugs? Because you're concerned?'

'Perhaps.'

'Do you ever think about me?'

'I thought you were okay.'

'How could I be okay? I wasn't helped and the men didn't stop. In the end my parents decided that the only option was to move away.'

'But when you came back I thought you were rebuilding your life. I heard you were at university.'

'Thought I was married with two kids living in Harrogate, did you?'

'Are you?'

'You're funny. You're not as kind as you were back then.'

'Tell me about Tereza and Laura.'

'I've already made a statement.'

'Your statement reads like an official press release.'

'What do you want?'

'I want you to reveal something.'

'Honestly, there's nothing.'

'Was Tereza your friend?'

'I was her boss, how could we be friends?'

'You're being cagey.'

'The other girls were her friends, why don't you talk to them?'

'We are. What's the significance of the tattoo on Tereza's foot?'

'I don't know.'

'Don't lie to me.'

'I'm not.'

'You have the same tattoo. I saw it just now.'

'We weren't friends exactly, but we got on. We went to the parlour together and thought it would be funny to have the same tattoo. That's all.'

'Why a scorpion? What does it mean?'

'It doesn't mean anything.'

'I want to help you.'

'Like you helped me last time?'

'Let's talk about Jeremy Brenton.'

'He's just a rich toff who comes to the club sometimes.'

'On his own?'

'With others.'

'Did he like Tereza?'

'I don't know.'

Gould left a pause. 'Is that all? Should I get someone to drive you back to Leeds?'

'I'm tired. I'd like to go home.'

'We dragged Tereza's body out of the river. Don't you care?'

'She had the right to kill herself. I respect her right to kill herself.'

'We don't know what happened to Tereza. Someone may have held her head under the water.'

'It's not fair to pile all this shit onto me. It's not my fucking fault.'

'Don't talk to me like that, girl. Shall I tell you what I have to do later? I have to ring Tereza's parents.' She just looked back at him. Tears had formed in her eyes. 'Not speaking now?'

'I want to go home.'

'Wait here.'

Gould went upstairs to Brown's office.

'How do you know her?' Brown asked.

'From seven years ago, when I was working in South Yorkshire. She was one of the girls being groomed and abused in Rotherham. She was twelve or thirteen. It was decided that a case couldn't be built and the crime wasn't even recorded. The abuse continued.'

'Rose has reported from the club,' Brown said. 'All the strippers are saying the same thing. Tereza was happy. Everyone is happy. They can't remember Laura. Brenton is a good fellow.'

'Sounds too good to be true.'

'Perhaps.'

Brown's computer screen was linked to the camera in the interrogation room. Brown and Gould watched Megan. 'Do you want to investigate her for drug use?'

'No. I think Megan just needs time to open up to me.'

'Drive her home yourself.'

•

'If this is a ploy,' Megan said, 'nothing will come of it. I'm not a fool. I know what you're doing.'

'What am I doing?'

The road was awash with water. Torrential rain beat against the windscreen and windows, adding to their sense of being cut off from the outside world.

'Trying to get me off guard so I'll say something.'

'So you do have something to say?'

'No. But if I did I'm not some naive girl who can be tricked into saying it.'

'Shall I take you to the club or to your home?'

'To my home please.'

'Where do you live?'

'I have an apartment here, in Micklegate.'

Gould drove down Fulford Road towards the town centre.

'Tell me about your current life, Megan.'

'My life? What do you want to know?'

'How are your parents?'

'My father died. I don't see my mother.'

'Why did you drop out of college?'

'It doesn't matter.'

Megan's phone bleeped. She lifted it from her bag and looked at the screen. 'It's a message from the policeman who interviewed me yesterday. Rose. He keeps messaging me. He wants to talk to me some more over a drink.'

She stretched out her arm to position the phone in front of Gould's face.

'Don't reply to him.'

'Does he work for you?'

'Yes.'

She looked through the spray at the taillights of the car in front. 'They still live locally. They're still abusing young girls.'

'I know.'

'It's as if they're untouchable. I'm over it… I've come to terms with the fact that you all said I was asking for it.'

'I never said that.'

'The detective who replaced you called me a slut in front of the child protection lady. She didn't contradict him. I couldn't understand. I had just told them how I was taken to houses where I was gang raped. I was thirteen. These were violent men, criminals, who were threatening to hurt my mum.'

Gould pulled the car into a parking place beside the curb and turned off the engine. He turned in his seat to look at Megan.

'You were let down.'

'You were the first officer to interview me. I trusted you. Where did you go?'

'I was a young officer, just starting out. They replaced me.'

'Why?'

'Does it matter?'

'It does to me.'

'I didn't agree with the party line.'

'The party line?'

'The view expressed by the other detective.'

'Anyway, I blame myself.'

'You weren't to blame, Megan.'

They were silent for a moment.

'Are you taking me home or what?'

He started the engine and re-joined the flow of traffic. After a pause he said, 'Have you thought about seeing a therapist?'

'I saw a therapist for a year.'

'Perhaps you should start again?'

'Relax. I'm just engaging in small talk to pass the time. Seeing you again brought it all back, that's all. I don't normally think about it at all.'

'Let's talk about the present. Are you in trouble, Megan?'

'No.'

They had reached Micklegate.

'I live over there.' He pulled up outside a handsome building with a white door. 'I have one of the top floor flats.'

'Promise you'll ring me if you want to talk?'

'I promise.'

Megan hesitated for a moment and then stepped from the car. Despite the rain she walked slowly to her door. Gould watched her in the rear-view mirror as he manoeuvred the car into the flow of traffic.

9

'Sorry to bother you on a Saturday,' Gould told Jeremy Brenton.

'No problem. Thank you for seeing me here rather than making me come to York.'

Brenton looked almost ordinary dressed in a grey sweater and jeans. He led Gould across the hall and into a living room at the rear of the house. A stocky young woman was sitting with two young children in the garden.

'Our new nanny,' Brenton said.

Gould nodded.

'My children are meant to be playing. I think they're frightened of her. I've yet to decide whether this is a good thing or not. Please take a chair, inspector.'

'This shouldn't take long.'

'Sorry that I've been less than completely honest with you. I tend to treat life as a game and can't resist playing the hand I'm given. In politics, if one is to flourish, one has to learn to be combative and arrogant. After a while, it becomes second nature. Besides, I was trying to protect my marriage.'

'You previously told us that the last time you saw Laura was in York at the end of May?'

'Yes, that's right.'

'So you were still seeing her when she was working at a nightclub in Leeds?'

'Yes. It's a club I go to when I'm in Yorkshire. Laura was looking for a job and I got her a position there. But only as a barmaid, not as a dancer.'

'You're a close friend of the manager?'

'We're friends, yes. We were contemporaries at Cambridge. Listen, before you ask me about high-class prostitutes, it's nothing unusual in the circles I move in.'

'I'm only interested in Laura, Mr Brenton.'

'The club's legit, and she only worked behind the bar. The last time I saw her she told me she had left the club and was working in a café.'

'There was a Czech girl at the club called Tereza. Did you know her?'

'No, I don't think so, but I can't claim to know all the dancers' names.'

'Are you planning to go back to the club?'

'I'm not actually.'

The door opened and a slender, brown-haired woman entered

the room. She was wearing shorts and her skin was tanned.

'Ah, this is my wife, Emma, inspector.'

Gould rose from his seat to shake Emma's hand. Emma smiled warmly, and sat down beside her husband. 'You look taken aback,' she said.

'No, it's just that from the way you've been described to me I was expecting…'

'A frail, nervous wreck?'

'Maybe not that bad.'

'Well, it's true that I haven't been well, but I'm quite better now.'

'I think it's more that I recognise you from somewhere.'

'My wife was an actress.'

'Back in the day,' Emma said. 'Under my maiden name, Harper.'

'Yes, I remember.'

'You want to ask me about Laura?'

'Yes. It would be helpful to know your opinion of her.'

'She was no good at looking after the children. She tried, but it's hard work and she was not much more than a child herself. She was quite shy. I think that could be mistaken for arrogance. But no, she was guarded and somewhat vulnerable.'

'So, you liked her?'

'Yes. You sound surprised?'

'It's just that you're describing a side to Laura's character that we weren't fully aware of.'

'Emma knows that I had an affair with Laura,' Brenton said, 'but she doesn't blame Laura.' He looked sadly at his wife. 'She's going to divorce me, but we've agreed to be civilised because of the children.'

'Is that why you sacked Laura?'

'No, Jeremy only told me about the affair a few days ago. I sacked Laura because she couldn't cope with the children. And I hated it, and felt guilty, because I sensed that Laura was looking for a home and a family.'

•

Gould arrived in Bordeaux in the early evening. After checking into the hotel recommended by Élodie, in the rue Lafaurie Monbadon, he made his way to the restaurant where they'd arranged to meet, in the place de la Bourse. He selected a table on the terrace with a view of the promenade and the river and ordered a whisky.

Bordeaux's manner was one of untroubled calm. The town centre, white shuttered and somnolent in the sunlight, was as self-assured and affluent as he remembered. Even the heat imposed itself with a kind of bourgeois elegance. All around there were young slim barelegged brunettes who looked like Élodie, and once or twice he mistook someone for her. When she finally appeared, wearing sunglasses, the warm breeze catching her hair, he wasn't sure that she was the right woman until she was almost upon him. She kissed him on each cheek and apologised for being late.

'I would have collected you at the airport.'

'No need. I caught a bus and then a tram.'

'How's the hotel?'

'Excellent. How are you? You sounded odd on the phone.'

'I'm fine. Really. Can we agree that once the food arrives we'll stop talking about the case?'

'Sure. We needn't talk about it at all.'

'I don't think we'll manage that.'

The waiter arrived. They ordered a bottle of wine.

'You first,' Élodie said.

'We investigated the nightclub in Leeds. Laura worked there as a waitress for two weeks. Brenton visits the club. He's a friend of the guy who runs the place. There's more. The girl we pulled from the river last month, and couldn't identify. She was a stripper at the club, a Czech girl called Tereza.' He told her about Megan and the shared tattoo.

'Have you brought Brenton back in?'

'I interviewed him in London this morning. His wife too. He was different from before.'

'In what way?'

'He was friendly and helpful. He recommended Laura for the waitress job. He didn't know Tereza. I believed him. I don't think there's anything suspicious here. Brenton's wife, Emma, knows that he had an affair with Laura. She's divorcing him.'

'Good for her.'

'Emma told me that she liked Laura and was sorry to let her go.

She said that Laura was shy and vulnerable, and that she tried to do a good job as a nanny.'

'That's new, and revealing.'

'In conclusion, I think it's unlikely that Laura's disappearance is connected to the club. I still think the Pariselle theory is more likely.'

A waiter brought the bottle. After the wine had been poured and tasted, Élodie said, 'Can you link Raymond Pariselle to Tereza?'

'Not as yet.'

'But you can link Brenton to both Laura and Tereza.'

'Yes.'

'If Pariselle knew Tereza there'd be pictures of her on his computer.'

'He could have erased them.'

'Not likely. Killers of women tend to keep their souvenirs. Anyway, aren't the tech guys looking for deleted files?'

'Let's keep an open mind either way. What's your news?'

'I've interviewed Camille Roche. Charles Roche turned up suddenly at my office and took me to see her. She identified the girl in the CCTV screenshot as Laura. She was very upset. I don't believe that Laura has gone off somewhere with her sister's knowledge.'

'Did you speak to Camille on her own?'

'No, her father wouldn't allow it.'

Children were running around the fountain of the Three Graces at the centre of the square.

'There's something else,' Élodie said. 'When I was last over, before I caught the flight home, I went to see Brenton's PA, Katherine.'

Gould shook his head. 'That was naughty, Élodie.'

'I wanted to ask her about the night she spent at the hotel with Laura.'

'Okay. What did she say?'

'She said that they were in a relationship. They slept together.'

'I didn't see that coming.'

Beyond the promenade, a cargo ship, carrying the fuselage of an aircraft, moved slowly upstream.

'Is it true that you're not coming back to York?'

'It's capitaine Bercot's decision.'

'What do you think?'

'I'd rather keep coming. But the capitaine has to manage resources and he has other priorities.'

'Even with a powerful figure like Roche breathing down his neck?'

'Roche still wants a low key investigation. It's one of the curious aspects of this case.'

Élodie's phone rang. 'I won't answer it.'

'You should.'

'Excuse me.'

Élodie walked away from the table and a little way into the square. Returning, she said, 'That was Camille. She wants to see me. At last we might be getting somewhere.'

'Where is she?'

'A few minutes away. She's coming here.'

'What are you expecting to learn from her?'

'I don't know. Something, without her father watching over her.'

The light was fading. Streetlamps spluttered into life. Beyond the elegant curves of the three bronze nudes, trams glided silently. A scooter pulled up at the curb. Camille, riding behind the driver, a boy, stepped down and made her way to the terrace. The scooter pulled away.

'I haven't got long,' Camille told Élodie.

'That's fine,' Élodie said. 'This is Tom Gould of the English police. Tom's leading the search for your sister in England.'

'I can't wait to tell you my news. I've received an email from Laura.'

'Really?' Élodie said.

'Yes. She's fine. She wants to be left alone, but she's fine. That's wonderful, isn't it?'

'Yes. When did you receive the email?'

'Today.'

'Have you told your parents?'

'No yet. They're out at some function. Is that any of your business? I thought I should tell you straight away since I know how much money and effort is going into finding my sister. I'm just so happy right now.'

'You sound more cross than happy,' Gould said. 'At least sit down for a few minutes, Mademoiselle.' He stood and pulled back a chair for her. She smiled and sat down beside him. 'Would you like a glass of wine?'

'I don't know.'

'Of course you do.'

'Just a sip.'

Gould lifted the bottle from the ice bucket and poured.

'Are you on a date?' he asked her.

'Oh, he's not my boyfriend.'

'Are you sure the email is from Laura?' Élodie asked.

'I knew you were going to ask that,' Camille said, angrily.

'Be reasonable,' Gould said. 'We have to ask.'

'Yes, I'm sure,' Camille said. 'It's from her Gmail account. And the way she writes… It's her. For a start she calls me Millie, and she's the only person who ever does that.'

'What does she say in the message?'

'She says she's fine. And that she's sorry. She didn't realise her disappearance would cause such a fuss. She says that she needs to be alone, and that she's not coming back until she's ready.'

'Can I see the message?' Élodie said.

'It's private.'

'I need to see it.'

Camille took out her phone and placed it on the table between herself and Élodie. She tapped options until the message appeared on the screen.

> Hello Millie, don't be cross. I'm fine. I needed to get away from everything and everyone. I'm sorry if you and others are worried. It never occurred to me that mum and dad would go to the police. Tell them I'm fine. I'm not going to tell you where I am because I don't want anyone to pester me. I'll come home when I'm ready. Please don't email me. I won't answer. I'm sorry if you think I'm being a bitch. I love you. Laura.

'Have you replied?'

'No. She says not to.'

Élodie passed the phone to Gould.

'Can I go now?'

'Not yet,' Gould said. 'Taste the wine. It's good.'

Camille took a sip of wine.

'Please forward the email to me,' Élodie said. 'My email address is on the card I gave you. Do you still have it?'

'Yes, of course I still have it.'

'Does the fact that she writes in English suggest that she's in England?' Gould asked.

'I don't know. It could do.'

'I think you should reply,' Gould said, 'if only to say how relieved you are and to ask her to occasionally contact you just to confirm she's okay.'

Camille nodded. 'If you think I should.'

'Can you forward the message to me now?' Élodie said.

Camille picked up her phone. 'Sent.'

The scooter had returned.

'If that's all…? I have a party to go to.'

'Celebrating?' Gould asked.

'It's my last night in Bordeaux. Tomorrow I'm going to the Med.'

'Have a good evening.'

'Thank you. You too. And thank you for the glass of wine.' As she stood she placed her hand on Gould's shoulder. She walked away across the square.

'What do you think?' Gould asked.

'I'm surprised.'

'Roche told us from the start that his daughter had simply decided to disappear.'

'Her mother didn't think so.' She smiled. 'The feeling of relief is euphoric.'

He nodded.

'So I guess this is the end of the investigation and of our time together. I won't have any excuse to return to York.'

He looked into her eyes. Then his glance shifted to her mouth and skin. Her breasts were partly revealed by the V-shape opening of her blouse. She looked away for a moment, and fingered her hair. Their eyes met again and they exchanged a nervous smile. 'More wine?' she said.

He ordered another bottle. Looking at her face, he could no longer see any trace of the police officer. He saw vulnerability and tenderness in her eyes and uncertain smile. He looked at the curve of her lips. The waiter brought the bottle and refilled their glasses.

'Bottoms up,' she said.

'Can I ask you something personal?'

'Of course.'

'Are you single?'

'Yes.'

'That's hard to understand.'

'Why? Because I scrub up well?'

'If you like.'

'Now you tell me something personal. It's only fair.'

'What would you like to know?' he said tentatively.

She thought for a moment. 'Are you sleeping with Karen?'

'No, of course not.'

'But at the cricket match…'

'We had a fling, months ago.'

'You ended it?'

'It should never have happened. She doesn't care.'

'She cares. Can you be so blind?'

'I'm not interested in Karen, Élodie. She works for me.'

'She's a good officer.'

'I know.'

'The boss treats her like a skivvy.'

'Yes, but he doesn't realise. He has no self-awareness. Karen has the guile to deal with the boss. Is it any better here?'

'No, it's the same.'

'You were promoted at a young age.'

'I'm well connected. My mother's retired, but she was a senior prosecutor in the judiciary here.'

They had finished the main course, and the second bottle. The terrace was packed. The table lights and hubbub of voices created the sense that they were sitting on a stage, or on the deck of a boat, such was the hot darkness of the night beyond. People were waiting to be seated. An elegant middle-aged couple emerged from the interior of the restaurant and walked between the tables.

'Putain, my mother and stepfather,' Élodie said. 'Perhaps they won't see us.' But Élodie's mother was already approaching their table.

'Élodie...'

Élodie rose to kiss her mother. 'This is Tom, a colleague.'

'A colleague?' she repeated.

'From England,' Gould said. He smiled broadly.

Élodie's stepfather had a strong handshake. 'Pierre and Marie,' he said.

'I didn't know you came here,' Élodie said.

'Would you like to join us for an aperitif?' Gould said.

Élodie shot him a look, and then, as Pierre and Marie sat down, kicked him under the table. 'We're running late so only have a few minutes,' Pierre said. 'Cognac?' He gestured to a waiter. 'How are you, chérie?' He leant forward and kissed Élodie on the cheek.

'I'm fine, papa.'

The drinks arrived.

Marie was looking at the two empty wine bottles. 'So you two are friends as well as colleagues?'

'Don't get your hopes up,' Élodie said.

'I see my daughter with a handsome man and I'm not allowed to hope?'

'Leave her alone,' Pierre said.

Marie smiled at Gould. 'My daughter is so defensive.'

'You're embarrassing him,' Élodie said.

'Are you embarrassed?'

'No.' He looked at Élodie and saw the pain in her eyes. 'But perhaps we should change the subject?'

'Yes,' Pierre said. 'Are you here working on a case?'

'Yes. We solved it today, hence this celebration.'

'The Roche girl?' Marie asked.

'Yes,' Gould said. 'She's been found.'

'That's confidential,' Élodie said.

Pierre looked at his watch. 'We should go.'

'I haven't finished my drink, darling,' Marie said.

'We're already forty minutes late.'

'I won't waste good cognac.'

Pierre lifted her glass and drank the cognac. 'There, problem solved.'

He stood and waited while his wife kissed Élodie goodbye. 'It was a pleasure meeting you,' she said to Gould. Gould and Pierre shook hands.

Élodie embraced Pierre. 'Please come over one Sunday,' he said. 'We miss you.'

'I will, papa.'

'I'm sorry about that,' Élodie said. 'Just bad luck.'

'I liked meeting them.'

'My mother wears me down.'

'Your stepfather has your back.'

'Yes. His love is unconditional.'

'When did they marry?'

'I was ten. You shouldn't have told my mother about Laura. She's a terrible gossip and they're clearly going to some society party. The news will be all over Bordeaux before Charles Roche finds out himself.'

'Sorry, I didn't think.' He took hold of her left hand and caressed her fingers with his thumb. 'Is this ok?'

'Yes.'

'We were having a good time, weren't we?'

'It doesn't have to end.'

•

Élodie invited Gould back to her apartment in the rue Notre Dame. They were both a little drunk. Away from the river the streets were silent. They turned into the Cours Xavier Amozan and strolled beneath the chestnut trees. An old lady was walking a poodle.

'Are you all right, Madame?' Élodie asked.

'It's too hot, ma petite, we can't sleep,' she told Élodie as she passed.

Élodie's shoulder brushed against Gould's arm. The lamplight projected an image of leaves against the shuttered façades. She walked slightly ahead. He touched the back of her bare thighs with his fingertips. She turned to embrace him and he pushed her against a car. The alarm went off and a light came on in one of the houses. They walked on, calmly, as if nothing had happened. She walked ahead of him again.

'Tie up your hair,' he said.

She lifted her hair away from her neck and tied it into an untidy chignon. He was close behind her. They came to the end of the alley of trees and turned into the rue Notre Dame.

•

Élodie opened the balcony windows. The spontaneity of their dance beneath the trees of the Cours Xavier Amozan had been replaced by a slight awkwardness. For a few moments they smiled at each other and circled around each other. 'Perhaps a nightcap?' Gould said.

Élodie fetched a bottle of whisky and they took turns drinking from the bottle.

'This is your third chance,' Élodie said teasingly.

'Is that right?'

'Yes. London, Paris and now Bordeaux.'

'I'm a bit thick.'

'So... What are you going to do now?'

Gould placed the bottle on a table and walked over to her. He kissed her, gently. Her eyes stayed open. He started to undo the buttons of her blouse, slowly and clumsily. She looked down at his hands. Then she looked up at him and smiled.

'Don't laugh at me,' he said. 'I want to do this right.'

He undid the last button. He slipped his fingers beneath the material and lightly touched one of her breasts. For several moments they stood stock still. Finally, she turned away and led him into the bedroom.

10

It was several hours before they slept. Gould woke first. He watched Élodie. A shaft of morning sunlight, streaming through a gap in the white drapes, revealed the minuscule fair hairs that lined the curve of her thighs and arms. He gently wiped her brown hair away from her face in the hope that she would wake, but she rolled onto her side, her sleep deep and calm.

He left a note for Élodie and went out to buy bread and croissants. Élodie was tidying the living room when he re-entered the apartment.

She was wearing the T-shirt Roche had given her. 'You're a member of team Roche now?'

'Why not? I'll make coffee.'

He followed her into the kitchen.

'You missed a call. Your phone lit up and I saw the name. Is Becky your wife?'

He frowned. 'Yes.'

Gould fetched his phone and then went out onto the balcony.

Élodie's phone bleeped. It was Roche.

'It must be a great relief for you,' Élodie said.

'Yes. Camille has just reached me. I know you saw her last night.'

'You were right all along.'

'Thankfully. We're having a little party tonight to celebrate. I'd like you to come.'

'I don't know.'

'You can bring Gould.'

'I can?'

'Of course. I want to thank both of you.'

'Can I get back to you?'

'I know you won't let me down. No need to bring anything, but it's formal so you'll need to dress appropriately.'

'Of course.'

'I'll see you tonight.'

Gould appeared in the doorway. When he reached for her she backed away. 'About last night,' she said. 'It was just one of those things, wasn't it? We don't have to make it into anything.'

'Well… okay. Is this because of my wife?'

'We're both adults. It doesn't have to change anything.'

'Whatever you want, Élodie.'

•

Cars were queuing the length of the dusty lane through the vines to the château.

'He said it was a little party,' Élodie said.

Half-an-hour later they reached the drive and were directed by a functionary to a narrow parking place beneath the trees.

Doors were flung open to create a route through the elegant rooms to the formal garden at the rear of the château. Lanterns lit the white walkways; waiters and waitresses in black uniforms held champagne flutes on silver trays.

Élodie noticed some eminent figures, including senior members of the judiciary and police, ballerinas from the Bordeaux opera, and a veteran TV newsreader. Among the great and the good of Bordeaux society there were many young people from the vineyard staff; and children ran and played between the trees.

Élodie introduced Gould to capitaine Bercot, and then, for an hour or more, they essentially kept to themselves, happy to be ignored; but when Élodie was spotted by people she knew she was pulled away into the crowd. Gould explored the outer edges of the garden and even walked out into the vineyard and down to the edge of the Garonne. Lights blinked far away across the dark water, and behind him, guarded by trees, the house was floodlit. Otherwise the darkness was absolute. Gould walked back, and skirted around the house, down steps to a lower level where there was a swimming pool. Young people had gathered here, with their own bottles of champagne. Gould had almost passed by when a girl called out to him. 'Monsieur…'

It was Camille. Gould walked over. 'I thought you were leaving Bordeaux today,' he said.

'My father asked me to stay for the party. I'll leave tomorrow.'

'How did he bring this together so quickly?'

'Oh, there was always going to be a party tonight. The annual summer bash. Is lieutenant Duquette here?'

'Yes. Somewhere.'

'Are you two together?'

'Together?'

'A couple.'

'What makes you say that?'

'Last night you looked like a couple.'

'Well… It's early days. I should get back.'

One of the other girls said, 'If you get bored, the real party starts here after midnight.'

Gould went back to the garden. He couldn't see Élodie. Bercot was standing alone so Gould went up to him and they began an awkward conversation.

Élodie was in the house. She had spent a few minutes looking at the paintings and the objets d'art in the second floor rooms, and now she was standing at the windows, looking down at the splendid summer garden, its geometric patterns outlined by the coloured lanterns. The scattered people were like actors on a stage. She smiled as she watched Gould and Bercot. Suddenly Roche was at her shoulder.

'Quite a sight, isn't it?'

'Yes.'

'Bercot and Gould look out of place.'

'I'm out of place too.'

'No you're not.'

A ghostly image of his face was reflected in the glass. She could not see his eyes. In an unconscious act of submission she placed her arms behind her back. But Roche had withdrawn and was sitting on a leather armchair.

'Mademoiselle…'

Élodie turned and went to sit in the chair opposite Roche.

'Here we are again,' she said.

'Quite.'

'It must be a great relief, hearing from Laura.'

He nodded. 'It has been a huge strain, particularly on my wife.'

'Is your wife here tonight?'

'No. She's in a sanatorium.'

'I'm sorry to hear that.'

'It always helps her. A few weeks of complete relaxation. I imagine you're checking the authenticity of the email?'

'Yes. But I have no reason to doubt that it was sent by Laura. The nicknames, the way the message is phrased… It's genuine. An imposter could not have achieved this.'

'That's reassuring.'

One of the waitresses entered the room with two glasses of

cognac. She placed the tray on the table beside Roche, smiled and made a silent retreat.

'Will you join me?'

'Yes.'

'My daughter said you and Gould looked intimate last night.'

She parted her lips in a half smile. 'I need you to be gallant, Monsieur Roche, I've drunk more champagne than is good for me.'

'I like to know everything,' Roche said. 'I'm not judging you morally. I'm questioning your judgment. What will your colleagues think? Will Bercot shrug his shoulders on the grounds that we all lose our judgment when it comes to sex? Bercot's a cold fish. And Brown? I watched you in his company. I know you respect him and want his approval.'

'It's nobody's business but mine.'

'Gould is married.'

'He's separated.'

'I don't think so.'

'Anyway, I'm not admitting that Tom and I are anything more than friends.'

'You can trust me to keep your secret.'

Roche leant forward and placed his sunburnt hand between Élodie's knees.

'Please stop.'

Roche removed his hand. He sat back in his chair. He emptied his brandy glass. 'It's your choice. I can wait.'

'You've been grooming me.'

'Grooming you? How old are you?'

'That's how it feels.'

'I think you're quite confused about what you want.'

'That's not true.'

'You should go back to the party.'

'Dismissed again,' Élodie said as Roche closed the door on her. She walked through the crowded ground floor reception rooms, searching for Gould. She found him in the library, a long rectangular room with polished parquet flooring. A spiral staircase gave access to a mezzanine. Lanterns shimmered beyond the windows, and figures moved in the shadows. At the far end of the room there was a large fireplace. Gould, alone in the room, was looking at the framed photographs on the mantelpiece.

'There you are,' Élodie said. 'Should we be in here?'

'There are pictures of Roche with Mitterrand and Mrs Thatcher. We've shown our faces. Can we go now?'

'Yes, let's go.'

•

It was the early hours when Gould and Élodie arrived back in Bordeaux. They went to Gould's hotel in the rue Lafaurie Monbadon since his stuff was there and he needed to leave for the airport only a few hours later. The night porter grinned at Gould when he asked for his key. 'I hate that,' Élodie said as they walked to the lift.

'Ignore him.'

As they entered the room Gould's phone rang. 'I have to take this.' He went into the bathroom and closed the door. Élodie sat on the bed. When he returned she said, 'Was that your wife?'

'Does it matter?'

'Last night you told me you were separated. Was that a lie?'

'It's complicated. We are in the process of separating.'

There was a long silence.

'I should pack,' he said.

'I'll drive you to the airport.'

'No, I'll take a taxi.'

Élodie went into the bathroom. Gould started to pack his belongings for the journey home.

11

Rose parked his car in a side street off Micklegate. He sent a text message to Megan: 'I'm in Priory Street. Come down for a chat or I'll haul you off to the police station for the day.'

Megan appeared ten minutes later. She opened the passenger door but didn't get into the car.

'Get in.'

'Please leave me alone. I've made my statement. I have nothing else to say.'

'Get in.'

'Leave me alone or I'll report you.'

'I won't tell you again.'

Megan stepped into the cabin and closed the door.

'Good. You don't know who I am do you?'

'What do you mean?'

'I don't just work for the police.'

Rose started the engine.

'Where are you taking me?'

'Just for a drive.'

'I haven't said anything.'

'Don't be frightened, I just want to talk.'

Driving out of York, Rose made sure that he kept to the speed limit.

'Who do you work for?'

'The same people as you.'

'Dan?'

'Further up the food chain.'

Rose left the city and headed north on country roads. For many minutes he didn't speak. Stone walls snaked across the low hills, white against vivid green, under a grey sky. The road climbed into the darkness of a wood.

'What's here? Where are we going?'

'Calm down.'

They hadn't passed another vehicle for miles. The sky was blocked by a canopy of mangled branches and leaves. Megan didn't know where they were. She took out her phone.

'What are you doing?'

'I want to make a call.'

'No. Put it away. Relax.'

He turned the car onto a track that cut between the tree trunks.

'I didn't say anything to Tom Gould.'

'I know, I read your statement.'

They were travelling deep into the forest. The car rocked as it sped along a dirt track that was mostly potholes and sunken tire tracks hidden beneath pools of brown water.

'Are you going to hurt me? Please, you're scaring me.'

Rose didn't answer.

'I need to pee.'

'You're like my ex-wife. Whenever we went anywhere in the car it was "I need to pee". She was worse than my little girl.'

'When your daughter grows up I hope she doesn't come across a man like you.'

'You don't know me.'

They rounded a bend and she saw the black Range Rover. A handsome man, instantly recognisable in black trousers and a tight white shirt, the cuffs rolled up, was leaning against the bonnet. He was looking at a mobile phone.

'What's he going to do?'

'He just wants to talk.'

Megan stepped down from the car and went over to the man. He didn't look up.

'Why have you brought me here, Dan? I've done nothing wrong.' She could smell his cologne.

'I'm watching the footage of our first time together. Come here and watch with me.' She could hear the laughter of the people watching and filming on their phones.

'No, I don't want to.'

'Come here.' He put his arm around her and held out the

mobile so that she could see.

'Why are you making me watch this?'

'To remind you. You belong to me.'

'Please Dan, I've done nothing wrong.'

'Each time the police questioned me about you I had my phone with me. The last time I placed it on the table. The evidence was right in front of them. They wouldn't help you then and they won't help you now. What did I tell you back then?'

'That you'd kill me if I went to the police again.'

'So?'

'I was interviewed because of a missing French girl. She was a waitress at the club. They're sniffing around because of that, not because of me.'

'The policeman who interviewed you drove you home. Why was that?'

'It was nothing.'

'I swear I'll beat you to death you this time.'

He was leaning against his car again. 'I need you to take a girl to Birmingham at the weekend.'

'I told you, I won't get involved in that.'

'You'll do this. I'll ring you the details on Friday. You better answer. Say it.'

'I'll answer.'

On the way back to the main road Rose said, 'You don't need to be scared of me. I like you. I liked you the moment I set eyes on you.'

'You work for Dan, he won't like that.'

'I don't work for Dan. He thinks he's king of the criminals, but he's just a backstreet punk. The people I represent are going to cut him loose and move their business out of Yorkshire for a while. I don't mind if you talk to Gould about Dan, but if you tell him about me, or mention Brenton or the name of any other client, I'll deny it and my friends will want to silence you. Do you understand?'

'Yes. I told him that you were calling me.'

'When?'

'When he drove me home after the interview. I didn't know who you were then. I just said that you'd left messages.'

'That's fine. You were right to tell me. So, have I made myself clear?'

'Yes.'

'I'm going out on a limb for you.'

•

On Friday Megan phoned Gould. She refused to go to the station so he told her he would pick her up on Skeldergate Bridge.

He could tell at once that she was scared. She ran to meet the car and opened the door before he had pulled to a halt.

'I lied to you,' she said.

'Do you want to change your statement? For that we'll need to go to the station.'

'I'll only talk off the record.'

'Off the record? I'm not a journalist.'

'You said you'd help me.'

'I will.'

'I don't believe you. Let me out.'

'I'll help you, but I can only do that if you tell me the truth.'

'I won't be taped, or sign a statement.'

'Okay.'

Gould parked below the bridge and took Megan to a café in Tower Street. She was in a daze so he held her shoulders and directed her into a booth beside the window. He asked the waitress for two cups of coffee and waited for her to bring them before looking at Megan and saying, 'So?'

'I'm still involved with him,' Megan said.

Gould nodded. She started to weep. He looked away and waited. She wiped her eyes with the back of her hand.

'I'm sorry. When my dad became ill we decided to move back to Yorkshire. Two years had gone by. I was seventeen. I didn't think he'd be interested in me anymore. And anyway I had a new name. I got a place at York University. One day he was just there, in his car, waiting outside the hall of residence like he used to wait outside my school. It was like I was thirteen again. I can't explain.'

'You don't have to explain.'

'He wanted older girls, more experienced, for sex parties with rich clients. He wanted me for that but also to work at the club and persuade other girls to go to the parties. I refused to get involved with the underage girls.'

'Tell me about the parties.'

'They're extreme.'

'Was Tereza one of the girls?'

'No. She was my friend. I wouldn't have done that to her.'

'Who are the clients?'

'Professional types mostly.'

'Jeremy Brenton?'

'No.'

'He's not one of the clients?'

'No.'

'The girls go willingly?'

'Yes. They can't resist the amount of money on offer.'

'The sex is consensual?'

'You can't enter that room and then say no.'

'Is the scorpion tattoo a kind of branding?'

'No, it's not connected. I was telling the truth when I told you it was something Tereza and I did on a whim.'

'Do you know what happened to her?'

'No, I swear.'

'You didn't talk about her with Dan?'

'No.'

'He didn't ask you about her?'

'No.'

'Is Salmon involved in all this?'

'No.'

'Laura Roche... Was she one of the girls?'

'No.'

'Where do these parties take place?'

'Private houses.'

'Drugs?'

'Yes. Cocaine.'

'And you persuade the girls to go? You offer and pay the money?'

'Yes, in cash. Dan gives it to me.'

'And you don't tell them about the nature of these parties?'

'No. My job is to get them in the room.'

'You're acting as the pimp. If Dan has covered his tracks, the only person I could arrest is you. Even if a case can be made and you testify against him, the law will want to punish you too.'

'I understand.'

'Last week you were holding your tongue about this. What has changed in the meantime?'

'Tomorrow I have to take a child to a house where she'll be abused. He's threatened to harm me if I don't. I won't do to her what was done to me.'

Gould was silent for a moment. 'I need time to work out what to do. In the meantime, I think you should get away from here, at least for the next few weeks. Where's your mother?'

'When dad died she went back to Cornwall. I can't go there. She blames me for everything.'

'I have a friend in Bordeaux. You should leave tonight.'

'Can we go straight to the airport from here?'

'You'll need your passport.'

'I don't want to go back to my flat.'

'If you're with me they can't hurt you, okay?'

'Okay.'

•

While they were in Megan's flat her mobile rang. 'It's him.'

'Answer it and go along with whatever he asks.'

'He'll know I'm lying.'

'I need to know the plan for tomorrow. The address. Put it on speaker.'

Megan placed the phone on the table.

'Hello, Dan.'

'Come to Rotherham at two tomorrow. Someone will meet you at Clifton park with the girl.'

'Yes, I'll be there.'

'Good.'

'Where am I to take her?'

'You'll be told tomorrow.' He ended the call.

'He's being careful,' Gould said. He looked at his watch. 'We have a long drive to Birmingham airport.'

'I'm ready.'

They were still in the city, driving down Tadcaster Road, when Gould became aware of the black Range Rover with tinted windows. It followed them onto the A64. Gould pulled over at the side of the road. The Range Rover did the same but at a distance. 'What's the matter?' Megan asked.

'Don't worry,' Gould said. 'Stay here.'

As Gould walked to the Range Rover he called the station and asked for backup. Dan's elbow protruded from the car. His fingers tapped the roof. A heavy gold watch fell a little way down his arm. Gould showed Dan his warrant card. Gould was surprised to find that Dan was alone in the car.

Dan stared unblinkingly into Gould's eyes. 'There's nowhere you can take her that I won't find her.'

'You were driving erratically. Have you been drinking or taking an illegal substance?'

'This will backfire on you.'

'Get out of the car.'

Dan jumped out of the cabin. Gould punched him hard just beneath his ribs. Dan cried out, like an animal, and fell forward against the car. Gould forced Dan's arms behind his back and snapped handcuffs on his writs; he then punched him in the side again, and pushed him down onto the floor. Dan, gasping in pain, remained still.

A police patrol car arrived. Gould greeted the two uniformed constables. 'He's a known thug from Sheffield. He was driving dangerously. He threw a punch at me so I had to pacify him. Do a breathalyser and check for substances. Hopefully you'll find something. Don't let him make a phone call.'

•

When Gould arrived back at headquarters, early the next morning, the desk sergeant told him, 'There was nothing in the car, we had to let him go.'

Gould nodded. Upstairs he phoned a colleague called Jenson in Rotherham and told him about the meeting at the park.

'Thanks for that,' Jenson said.

'You going to do anything?'

'What do you think? It's been a while, we should go for a pint.'

'Why's that?'

Gould ended the call and checked his email. There was a message from Élodie: 'I met Megan at the airport and drove her to the beach house. She can use it for as long as she likes. Are you going to tell me what this is about? Are you going to fly out at the weekend? Love, Élodie.'

Gould typed: 'Thanks for helping her. I'll tell you about it when I see you. Can't come this weekend.'

A reply arrived almost at once. 'Okay.'

12

Just after Élodie had clicked 'send' she received a call from Charles Roche asking her to meet him for a drink after work. She said yes without a moment's hesitation. She spent the morning at headquarters, catching up on paperwork.

She went down to the canteen to find Bercot sitting with Brown at a corner table. Bercot waved her over. She smiled at Brown. 'What are you doing here?'

Brown was on his annual holiday, travelling with his wife to Spain. 'We like to have at least one week in the sun,' Brown said. 'Since we were passing through Bordeaux I thought I'd introduce myself to capitaine Bercot and surprise you.'

Élodie sat down opposite Brown. 'It's good to see you,' she said.

'Bercot and I have been arguing about Jonny Wilkinson.'

'Jonny Wilkinson?'

'The rugby player.'

'Not arguing, debating,' Bercot said.

'I think he was a one trick pony but Bercot thinks he was a philosopher. He played for Toulon, Bercot's hometown.'

Bercot shrugged. 'That has nothing to do with it.'

'Good news about the Roche girl,' Brown said.

'There are lessons to learn,' Bercot said.

'I agree,' Brown said.

'Too much of my budget for the last month was wasted on this.'

'If you mean sending me to England,' Élodie said, 'the only expense was the travelling. I stayed at a friend's flat.'

'What was the name of that posh hotel in London, Élodie?'

'Okay, except for that.'

'You should have put that claim in the bin,' Brown said.

'I've invited capitaine Brown to lunch. You'll come?'

'Of course.'

'I'll go and book a table.'

'Book a table? Let's go to one of the places near here.'

'I'm not taking a foreign guest to a corner bistro.'

After Bercot had departed Élodie said, 'This is going to take up most of the afternoon.'

'I like him,' Brown said.

Élodie nodded.

'Now we're alone I have something to ask you. It may not matter now, but the woman who works for Jeremy Brenton says you went to her flat in London and asked questions about Laura. Is that true?'

'Yes that's true.'

'Did I ask you to do that?'

'No. I'm sorry.'

'She's made an official complaint of harassment through Brenton's lawyer. I'll deal with it.'

'Are you going to issue a press statement about Laura? Have you spoken to capitaine Bercot about it?'

'We've agreed to issue a statement just saying that she has contacted her family.'

Élodie nodded, but remained silent.

'You don't agree?'

'It's not that. I'll feel happier when I actually see her.'

•

Élodie walked to the quai du Maréchal Lyautey. People were strolling or sitting in small groups, enjoying the evening sunlight. A dance club had set up a small sound system on the quay. Within a vague circle of onlookers couples were dancing a Lindy Hop to Glen Miller's 'In the Mood'. Holding hands, these disparate couples – for they weren't matched in terms of age, height, ability or gender – kicked, swivelled, hopped and pirouetted at the same time as pulling each other together and then apart in a flurry of playfully flirtatious but innocent movement. If it can be possible for a human being to be as happy as a dog fetching a ball, this came close.

It was only after several minutes that Élodie realised that one of the better dancers, a slim man in a loose white shirt and navy trousers, was Roche. At the next break in the music he spotted Élodie and walked over.

'Surprised?'

'Yes.'

A new tune started up. Roche took hold of Élodie's hand. 'Come on.'

'No.'

'It's not difficult. It's improvised. Just move to the music. You'll have fun, I promise you.'

Roche was already pulling her into the circle. An hour went by. Yellow lamps glowed against the gathering blue of the sky, along the promenade and across the Pont de Pierre.

Roche took Élodie to a quiet spot in the garden that formed a road of green through the promenade. 'That was fun,' Élodie said.

'Good.'

'How did you get involved?'

'My wife wanted us to join the club, to have something to do together. I agreed for her sake, thinking that I'd detest everything about it, but the opposite happened. My wife soon lost interest; but I found it liberating. It helped me through a period of terrible depression. Now it's one of the ways I fight against the onset of old age. Can I ask you something?'

'Of course.'

'Was Laura sleeping with Brenton?'

'I can't answer that.'

'I think you just have.'

Out of nowhere a young woman appeared with a bottle of Krug Champagne in an icebox.

'Thank you, Marianne,' Roche said. 'Please tell Paul to leave the car in the garage. I'll drive myself tonight.'

'Yes, sir.' The girl withdrew.

'To celebrate and to thank you,' Roche said, releasing the cork by twisting the bottle. He filled the two flutes.

'Clos du Mesnil 2000,' Roche said. They clinked glasses. Élodie took a sip and made sure she tasted the wine in her mouth before swallowing. Roche emptied his glass. 'It's not red wine. You're allowed to drink it like water. It works best when you knock it back. Think of swallowing an oyster.'

'You want me to empty my glass too?'

'How else can I refill it?'

Roche looked at the arc of Élodie's throat as she swallowed the wine. She wiped her mouth with the back of her hand and smiled.

Roche reached for the bottle and refilled the glasses. Soon the bottle was empty. Roche thrust it upside down in the ice bucket.

'Do you expect me to go somewhere with you, Monsieur Roche?'

'If you like I can take you to my apartment. But I have to leave for the airport before midnight.'

'I don't think so. Am I not worth a whole night?'

'I didn't plan things this way. I only learned after I called you that I have to go to Paris tonight.'

'If I go with you what happens afterwards?'

'You'll become my mistress.'

'I won't become your mistress.'

'He doesn't deserve you.'

'Who?'

'Gould.'

'You're playing me,' Élodie said. 'First you soften me up with the dancing, making me think that you have a heart; second, you treat me like a prostitute to put me in my place.'

'You're overthinking.'

For a moment they were silent.

Élodie heard herself saying, 'Laura told Brenton's PA that she felt unloved by her parents.'

She watched his eyes narrow. 'That's nonsense. It's the kind of thing she liked to say to get back at me.'

'Get back at you?'

'For not being her real father. For being too strict and too demanding. I don't know. You tell me. You were a teenage girl once.'

'I love my stepfather. When I was going through the difficulties of adolescence I hid from him things that would have worried or hurt him.'

'I wonder if that's how he remembers it.'

'Well, I tried anyway. We were discussing Laura.'

'Is this the Champagne talking, or are you working right now? Which one of us is actually being played?' He looked at his watch.

'And now I should go. Are you coming or not?'

He stood and held out his hand. She shook her head. 'I'll stay here. Thank you for a lovely evening.'

She watched him walk away.

•

At first Élodie thought the beach house was empty. She placed her keys on the table and went to the terrace to see if Megan was on the beach. It was early in the morning. The sun had yet to break through the clouds. The beach was as vacant as a winter field.

'Hello.'

Startled, she turned to see Megan. She looked as if she had risen from bed in a hurry. 'You shocked me.'

'Sorry.'

'Did I wake you?'

'No. What's wrong? Why are you angry?'

'I'm not.'

Megan followed Élodie back inside. Élodie could hear someone moving behind the bedroom door. 'Oh. You have a man here.'

'Is that ok?'

'Yes. I won't stay. I only came to check that you were okay.'

The bedroom door opened and Rose walked through. 'Hello Élodie.'

'What's going on?'

Rose placed his arm around Megan's waist and kissed her hair.

'We're together.'

Megan rested her head against Rose's chest. Élodie watched them for a moment.

'Tom didn't tell me.'

'Tom doesn't know.'

'It's only just happened,' Megan said. 'You don't need to tell him.'

'Why's that?'

'It's my life,' Megan said.

'You don't like me, do you?' Rose said.

Élodie took out her phone.

'Okay, tell him, I don't fucking care,' Megan said. Megan and Rose went outside.

Gould didn't pick up so Élodie left a message: 'Kevin Rose is here. He spent the night with Megan.'

Rose reappeared. 'Told Gould?'

'Yes.'

'Good.'

13

Rose arrived at work on Monday morning to find Gould waiting for him in the car park. 'We need to talk,' Gould said.

'We do.'

Rose followed Gould to the stairwell at the back of the building and into a basement storeroom. He closed the door. As Rose turned Gould punched him hard in the stomach. Rose fell back against a column of boxes, and then slumped onto his knees, bent over in pain. He glanced up at Gould. 'That hurt,' he said. 'It's a good thing I deserve it.'

'Why's that?'

'Because I'll let it go. Things could quickly get out of control. You're not a violent man, not really. I am.'

Gould's fists were clenched. 'Come on, then, Rose, fight back. I won't pull rank.'

Rose leant back against the boxes. He took out a cigarette and lit it with a lighter. 'I really like her,' he said.

'Is that right?'

'Yeah. I admit I took advantage. I'm surprised to discover that I like her, but it's true.' Rose shrugged.

'How long do you expect it to last?'

'I don't know.'

Gould sat on a crate. For a few moments neither man spoke.

'Listen,' Rose said, 'don't take this the wrong way, but do you want her yourself?'

'Of course not.'

'So what is this about?'

'She's a suspect. You know the rules.'

'You're too worked up for it to be just that. She told me her story. You feel responsible in some way. You never did what was necessary to protect her. Because to do what's necessary means breaking the rules and more.'

'And you're the man for that?'

'I think you know I am.'

'What are you saying, Rose?'

'I know more about Dan and his world than you. I'm going to fix this once and for all.'

Gould stood up. 'I'll leave you to your fantasies. If I hear you've harmed Megan we'll have this talk again.'

'If you say so, tough guy.'

Gould grimaced and paused.

'Why does nobody around here have a sense of humour

anymore?' Rose said.

'When is Megan coming home?'

'Tomorrow. I know Megan told you about the prostitution ring. Now that we know that Laura Roche was not involved in this, and is unharmed, we can let it go, right? Vice won't be interested. They'll know already.'

'I haven't decided what to do.'

'We both know that the only person we could charge is Megan.'

'I don't want to see you for a while. Take some leave.'

'I've exhausted my interest in this backwater. I'm going to transfer back to vice.'

'Good. I'll fast-track the paperwork.'

'We've been friends. I regret ending things like this.'

'I regret it too.'

•

The farm was located on the remote uplands of the Moors, its derelict buildings hidden from any road. Rose drove down a long private farm track. Beyond the channels of mud and scraps of heathland illuminated by the car's headlamps the landscape was a black nothingness.

When he pulled into the yard the lorry was already there, and the others were waiting in the cone of light thrown by an overhead spotlight. Stanković's dog was walking a circle at the edge of light. Stanković and Rose shook hands. 'Everything's ready,' Stanković said.

'Thanks for doing this,' Rose said.

'My pleasure.'

Ice-cold air drifted from the container, visible as a mist in the artificial light. Inside the container, the carcasses of pigs dangled from hooks. At the front, three naked men were standing on wooden crates, straining desperately as the ropes that connected their necks to the roof of the lorry tightened. Their swollen faces were contorted and bloody. Blood-spattered plastic sheeting covered the floor and sides of the container.

'Did you learn anything from them?' Rose asked.

'They don't know anything,' Stanković said.

'Has the plan changed?'

'No. I'm going to spend time with my family in Serbia. We'll wait for you to tell us when this district is viable again.'

Rose nodded. He looked at the hanging men. 'Hello Dan,' he said.

'Can we get on with this?' one of the men said.

Stanković nodded. He turned to Rose. 'Do you want to do it?'

'No.'

'Are you sure?'

'Yes.'

Stanković climbed into the van and kicked away the crates.

Rose watched until the hanging legs stopped kicking. He nodded at Stanković and walked back to his car. Behind him, Stanković's men were already wrapping the corpses in the plastic sheeting.

•

‘Can I come in?’ Gould said.

‘It’s late,’ Élodie said; but she let him in and closed the door. ‘How did you know I was back in York?’

‘Karen saw you in the street. She waved but you kept walking.’

‘I didn’t see her.’

‘Why haven’t you come to the station?’

‘I’m not here for work. I’m on leave.’

He followed her into the living room.

‘I’ve been drinking my friend’s whisky,’ she said.

‘Your friend?’

‘The owner of this apartment. Would you like some?’

‘Yes.’ She poured a measure into her glass and fully stretched out her arm to hand it to him.

‘Are you tipsy?’

‘A little.’

Gould took hold of her hand and pulled her into an embrace. He hugged her tightly. She rested her head on his shoulder, but didn’t reciprocate. He wanted to kiss her but her head stayed on his shoulder, her face turned away.

She gently pushed herself free. ‘Can we just talk?’

‘Of course.’

‘How’s Megan?’

'I didn't come here to talk about Megan.'

'I want to know.'

He frowned. 'She's with Rose.'

'He's serious about her?'

'I don't know.'

She left a pause. 'She's old enough to make her own decisions.'

He emptied his glass. 'I want to tell you about my wife.'

'Please, Tom, it's none of my business.'

The heat was stifling. She stood before the open windows with her back to him. She scratched the back of her neck. 'Raymond's restaurant is dark,' she said. 'It's closed.' She looked further along the quay. 'His house is up for sale. It's true, isn't it, that we never really know anyone?'

Gould's phone rang.

'Your wife?'

'No. Work.'

Gould answered the call. 'Where? I'm on my way.'

'What is it?'

'A roadside shooting. I have to go.'

'Okay. Can I come?'

•

The car, an Aston Martin, was parked at the side of the country road, illuminated by the headlamp beams of two patrol cars. The road cut through a wood.

Gould parked his car at the perimeter and walked across the road. Élodie followed.

'How long before the team get here?' Gould asked one of the constables.

'Shouldn't be long now, sir.'

'Hello, Mike,' Élodie said.

'Ma'am.'

She was looking at the side window of the car. It was splattered with blood and pieces of skull and brain.

'It can't have been easy to find this.'

'No.'

'What have you done so far?' Gould asked.

'I opened the door to check that he was dead, that's all.'

'You felt for a pulse?'

'Yes.'

'Was the engine still running?'

'Yes.'

'So you turned it off?'

'I don't know. Yes. I must have.'

'Get a grip. What else?'

'Sorry. That's it. I opened the door. Felt for a pulse. Turned the engine off.'

Gould opened the driver's door. The victim was slumped over the driving wheel.

'Shot in the head,' Gould told Élodie.

She looked over his shoulder into the cabin. Then she touched his shoulder to make him look at her. 'It's Brenton,' she said.

Gould looked more closely at the man and saw that Élodie was right.

Gould searched the man's jacket pockets. 'Nothing,' he said. He turned to the constable. 'Who called this in?'

'A member of the public who was driving by. He wasn't here when we arrived. The operator asked him to wait but he was distressed and wanted to get home. We have his details. I don't think he saw anything other than the car.'

Élodie came over. 'What was he doing out here?'

'Brenton has a holiday home in Yorkshire so perhaps he was going there.'

'He was executed.' Élodie looked at the car. 'Wait a minute…'

'What?'

'The passenger door is open. Don't you think it's surprising that he was on his own?'

Élodie walked around the car. 'The grass at the kerb has been flattened.' She could see where someone had left a trail through the grass and into the wood.

She scrambled down into a shallow ditch and then into the wood. She could see a body lying a little further ahead.

'Over here,' she shouted.

'Élodie, wait.'

A woman was lying on her stomach. Élodie gently moved her onto her side, relieved to discover that she was alive. She wiped the woman's hair away from her bloodied face. There was a wound on her forehead. Her eyes were closed and she was groaning. 'It's okay, Kate,' Élodie said. 'It's going to be okay.'

A torch beam glided across Kate's face as Gould approached. 'She has a gash in her head, but she hasn't been shot,' Élodie said. 'I think she's in shock.'

She cradled Kate's head in her lap.

'She ran,' Gould said. 'She was lucky.'

'The wound is at the front, so I think she fell and hit her head.'

Gould phoned Karen. 'Sorry to wake you. I need you to come in.'

They could hear a siren. A few moments later the flashing lights of an ambulance swept between the black trees.

•

Karen was sitting at her desk in the incident room.

'It's good to see you,' Élodie said.

'Are you back with us?'

'No, I'm not working.'

The two women looked at Gould.

'I was with someone when you phoned…' Karen said.

'Good for you,' Gould said.

'…but I came running. You could at least try to be nice.'

'I'll get us some coffees from the machine,' Élodie said. She went out into the corridor.

'Was Brenton on the way to his holiday home?' Gould asked

Karen.

'It's near Howsham, so yes, probably.'

They sat in silence for a few minutes.

'Why did you call me in? What can we do tonight?'

'Can you check for any CCTV in the vicinity.'

Élodie came back with the coffees.

'I need to make some phone calls,' Gould said. He went into Brown's office and closed the door.

'I was going to email you today,' Karen told Élodie. 'I need to show you something.'

They sat together in front of Karen's computer.

'I was taking a final look at the York station CCTV footage.' The footage showed people walking along the platform beside a train. 'This was taken later in the evening. These people are boarding a train bound for London.' She pointed at a slim blonde. 'I think this girl could be Camille.'

'Could you freeze the frame?'

Élodie looked closely at the image.

'I've only seen a photograph of Camille,' Karen continued, 'so I wasn't sure. And I don't suppose it matters now, anyway.'

'It is Camille,' Élodie said.

'It is?'

'I think so.'

'What does it mean?'

'I don't know. Perhaps we'll never know what these girls have been up to. Something weird is going on in that family. Good work, though. Have you shown Tom?'

'Yes. He's been distracted and bad-tempered. I don't think he was interested.'

'You should go home. Tom didn't need to call you in.'

'It's almost light. I won't get back to sleep.'

'Won't your boyfriend be missing you?'

'I don't have a boyfriend.'

'I thought you said…'

'I picked him up in a bar.'

'Well if you like him you should get back to him.'

'I told him to leave.' She shrugged.

'We've all been there.'

'I'm going to request a transfer.'

'A transfer? Why?'

'I feel trapped.'

'Have you spoken to the chief?'

'Yes. More than once. He's not supportive. He wants to keep me where I am indefinitely. But it's not just that. I'm not getting on with Rose.'

Élodie nodded.

'Things used to be okay between us. His ribbing would always be more like baiting, if that makes sense, but recently… I don't know…'

'What?'

'Sorry, I shouldn't be telling you this.'

'Please, I want to know.'

'The point is I've been here too long and need to leave if I'm going to get anywhere.'

'Listen, if Rose is harassing you…'

'It's not important. I shouldn't have said anything.'

Gould came back into the room. 'I've contacted the NCA. I need to stay to hand things over when they arrive, but you two should go home.'

'I'll stay,' Karen said.

'The girl in the CCTV is Camille,' Élodie said.

'Are you sure, because I'm not.'

'I'm sure.'

'What difference does it make?'

'I'd like to know why Camille lied.'

'If you're thinking of questioning Camille again, you should discuss with Brown and Bercot first.'

'Oh, they'll take the same line as you.'

'It's up to you.'

'And Brenton? We thought the investigation was closed, but it seems to be opening up again.'

'I doubt that. Whatever Brenton was mixed up in it wasn't connected to Laura.'

'I saw Charles Roche a few days ago. He asked me about Brenton. He wanted to know whether Brenton had been sleeping with Laura.'

'You're not seriously suggesting that Roche has people killed?'

'No, not seriously.'

They were silent for a few moments.

'If you have to wait here for the NCA officers, shall I go to the hospital to talk to Katherine?'

'Yes, but take Karen.' He took Élodie to one side. 'Can we meet up later?'

'Yes.'

•

It was early morning when Élodie and Karen arrived at the hospital.

'Physically, she's stable,' a doctor told them. 'She's suffered a knock to the front of her head. We've stitched the wound and she's had a scan. Nothing to worry about but we want to keep her in overnight. She's very upset, of course. A councillor will talk to her when she's ready. I've given her a sedative.'

'So we can talk to her?'

'Yes, but just for a few minutes.'

Katherine was sitting up in bed. Her face was pallid and she had been crying.

'This is Karen,' Élodie said.

'I'm scared,' Katherine said.

'I know, but you're safe here. There's a policeman sitting outside the room. And we don't think you're in danger.'

'Why would anyone kill Jeremy?'

Élodie sat on the bed. 'Is it okay to talk about what happened?'

'We were driving to his cottage. A motorbike overtook us and then flagged us down. Jeremy stopped the car. The rider got off the bike and walked back to us. He lifted his arm and shot Jeremy through the windscreen. I got out of the car and ran. I think I tripped over something. The next thing I remember is you, looking down at me.'

'Did the rider chase you and shoot at you?'

'No, I don't think so.'

'Can you remember anything about the way he looked?'

'He was in his twenties. He had a beard.'

'Surely he was wearing a helmet?'

'I think he took his helmet off. I think he wanted Jeremy to know who he was. He waited a few seconds before he fired.'

'You're sure?'

'Yes. He was standing in the headlamp beams. I saw his face.'

'Okay. Thank you. Was there anything unusual about the way Jeremy was behaving? Was he worried about anything?'

'No, nothing.'

'You can tell me anything, Kate.'

'There's nothing to tell. If you want me to say that Jeremy was a bit of a shit, well, yes, but then you already know that. But that's all he was.'

'What about Charles Roche?'

'Charles Roche? I don't know who that is?'

'Laura's father.'

'I've never met him. Why mention him?'

'Jeremy knew him though?'

'They met once or twice in London.'

'When did they last meet?'

'A couple of nights ago.'

'Were you there?'

'No, I wasn't there. I just want to get out of here.'

'Do you want me to call someone? A family member or friend?'

'No.' Katherine looked at Karen. 'Why doesn't she speak? Who is she?'

'She's a colleague. We'll let you get some rest.'

•

The next day was Brown's first back in the office. Tanned and wearing a light blue shirt, he started the day in a relaxed mood, despite the fact that Karen hadn't turned up for work.

The large screens in the meeting room displayed the York station CCTV footage. Gould briefed Brown on Brenton's killing and the arrival of the NCA officers.

'It's out of our hands,' Brown said.

'It could come back to us.'

'I'm not interested in Brenton,' Brown said.

'But in the context of our investigations, Brenton remains a question mark,' Élodie said.

'I don't agree,' Brown said. 'Why are we looking at the screens?'

'These images were taken at the station later on the evening that

Laura returned to York. I think the woman in these images is Camille.'

Brown put on his spectacles and glared at the screens. 'Could be anyone.'

'No, it's her.'

'So they were both in York that evening. What does that change? I think they've have been playing some kind of game. We could charge them with wasting police time, but what would be the point?'

'It puts a doubt in my mind,' Élodie said. 'We need to question Camille about it. I don't think the case should be closed until we see Laura.'

'What do you think?' Brown asked Gould.

'I trust Élodie.'

Brown was silent for a few moments. 'It's up to you Élodie but perhaps you should discuss with Bercot first.'

'Thanks, that's all I wanted.'

As they were walking back down the stairs, Élodie asked Gould, 'Where's Karen? Is she sick?'

'I don't know. She hasn't phoned in.'

He took out his phone and rang her number. There was no answer, but a minute later she called him back.

'I'm sorry,' she said, 'I've been vomiting all night. I won't be in today.'

'You could have called earlier.'

'I'm sorry.'

'Okay.'

14

Rose walked into the incident room. Karen looked away, and it was as if she was trying to shrink her body into a protective ball.

'How are you doing?' he asked, his tone completely normal.

'Go away,' she said quietly.

'Be like that.'

Gould came out of Brown's office. 'Karen, can you join us?'

Karen circled round Rose to get to the office.

'Clearing your desk?' Gould asked Rose.

'Yes. My transfer to Leeds came through. Thanks for expediting it.'

'South Yorkshire tell me that the relatives of Megan's abusers have reported them missing.'

'Yes. They could be the victims of a turf war; or perhaps they've left the country and returned to their ancestral village. It's good news for Megan and countless young girls in Yorkshire.'

'Yes. I'll buy you're a drink sometime.'

Gould shook Rose's hand and then went back into the office and closed the door. Rose watched Brown, Gould, Élodie and Karen through the glass.

'We're concerned about you,' Gould said to Karen. 'You were off sick for a week and since you've been back you've been quiet and withdrawn.'

'Have I done something wrong? Am I being reprimanded, sir?' Karen asked.

'No, of course not.'

'I shouldn't be here,' Élodie said.

'No, I want you to stay,' Karen said.

'Are you still ill, is that it?'

'No, I'm not ill, sir.'

'So why are you so sullen all the time?'

'I didn't know I was. I'll try harder to be merry, sir.'

'Cut out the "sirs", Karen.'

'I want a transfer,' Karen said suddenly. 'I want a transfer this week, otherwise I'll resign.'

Brown had been reading some papers rather than fully concentrating on the conversation. He now looked up and stared at Karen. 'A transfer to where?' he asked.

'I don't care. Anywhere.'

'I don't think so. And don't complain about being held back. You're only a girl.'

'I'm only a girl? Would you say to a man of my age "You're only a boy"?'

'I only meant that you're very young and have plenty of time.'

'You need to go on a course to learn about sexism.'

Brown brought his fist down hard on the desk, causing his pens to jump in the air. 'Don't you dare talk to me like that,' he shouted.

Karen just stared back at him.

Rose knocked on the door and entered the office. 'What is it?' Brown snapped.

'Sorry to disturb you,' Rose said. 'I'm on my way out. I just wanted to tell Karen I'll see her soon.'

Karen stood and almost tripped as she rushed from the office. Rose exited too, but casually.

'What's going on with her?' Brown said.

'I don't know,' Gould said.

'Karen told me recently that she wasn't getting on with Rose,' Élodie said.

'Well, it doesn't matter now,' Gould said. 'He's leaving us.'

Élodie went to find Karen. She was sitting at her desk.

'Rose is leaving,' Élodie said.

'He is?'

'Yes.'

'Good.'

Élodie left a pause. 'Karen, what's happened?'

'Nothing. Nothing. Please, Élodie, I'm fine.'

•

Rose drove to Micklegate. Megan was sitting at her kitchen table, leafing through the pages of a textbook.

'I'll help you pack,' he said.

'Pack?'

'Your stuff. I want you to move in with me today.'

Megan took off her glasses and stood nervously with her hands behind her back.

'I'm sorry, but I tried to tell you before. I don't want to move in together. I'm sorry if you're disappointed.'

'You're sorry if I'm disappointed?'

'Yes.'

'I thought we had an agreement. I've gone out on a limb for you.'

'I know. And I'm grateful.'

'I don't think you do know. How do you think I solved your problem?'

'I don't know. I don't want to know.'

'How will you afford to live here now that you no longer work at the club? I won't support you if we don't live together.'

'I'll get a parttime job in a restaurant or bar, like other students. I want to support myself.'

'Now that you've manipulated me to get what you want.'

'I haven't manipulated you. You took advantage of me. You did what you wanted without caring whether I wanted it or not.'

'So, you think the debt's been paid?'

'You're not going to hurt me, are you? Because you look like you want to.'

'I'm not going to hurt you, Megan.'

'Please understand. I want to be your girlfriend. But I want to live on my own, at least to start with. Men have been controlling me all my life. It's important to me to control my own life.'

Rose thought for a moment. He allowed his expression to soften. 'Okay. I can understand that.'

'You can?'

'I won't pretend that I'm not disappointed. But I'll give you the time you need.'

•

Rose took Megan to a windswept bluff where the moorland's carpet of purple heather was threadbare. Stretches of heather had been burned to leave black patches or to reveal white rocks that looked like bones. A forest of pines covered one side of the valley. There were no stonewalls and no livestock. They met no other cars on the single lane road.

'Have you ever been here?' Rose asked.

'Never.'

'I told you I'd take you to a place that was remote,' Rose said. 'Bleak is beautiful in my book.'

'It is beautiful.'

'There's a footpath that will take us through the forest. On the other side there's a view of the whole valley.'

Rose turned the car onto a farm track that cut through the moor. He drove to the treeline and parked. He turned in his seat to look at Megan.

'What?' she said.

'Nothing.'

They stepped out of the car.

'Stay there for a moment,' Rose said. 'I'll get my coat from the boot.'

Rose opened the boot. A baseball bat and a spade lay on a plastic sheet. He contemplated the bat for a few moments.

Megan was standing a few steps away from the car with her back to him.

'Don't turn around,' he called. 'I have something for you. A surprise.'

He lifted the bat from the boot and walked towards Megan. He raised the bat, looking at the back of Megan's head. He looked at her head for a long time. He sensed that she was about to move. 'Don't fucking turn round.'

He took a stride forward. The wind caught her hair, lifting it away from her neck. His arm started to shake. He felt nauseous. He lowered his arm and let the bat rest against his leg.

'Are you still there?' she said.

Rose walked back to the car. He dropped the bat in the boot. He no longer felt sick.

'You know what,' he said, 'I've changed my mind. I'm hungry. Let's find a pub.'

Megan turned. 'All right. What was the surprise?'

'A present. I thought it was in the boot.'

The rain fell heavily. The path was awash with muddy water.

'Let's go,' he said.

PART THREE

15

Gould and Élodie caught a flight to Hyères. They hired a car at the airport and followed the winding coast road, the cobalt blue Mediterranean on their right, the green densely vegetated hills of the Maures on their left. Some of the hillsides were cut into Cubist shapes by hundreds of white villas; but, then, on the other side of a high bend, there was only the natural world, an ancient landscape of black branches and rust red earth glimpsed between the rocks. A sailing boat with an orange sail glided away from the rocky shoreline like an arrow. The cries of children and laughter of girls drifted on the air from hidden beaches and luxury yachts. Élodie's hair was dishevelled by the pine scented breeze. Gould told her that she looked glamorous in her Persol sunglasses, especially when she smiled. He felt the pleasure of the northerner on arriving in the South.

They headed inland and followed the road to Gassin. Here they spent the night in a small hotel at the top of the village. From their window, beyond the bay of Saint-Tropez, a blue parking lot for white boats, the hills lay against the sky in layers of diminishing clarity. They woke in a white walled room between white sheets. With the windows open, daggers of light sliced through the slats of the grey green shutters. Élodie checked her phone. 'There's a message from Camille,' she said. She climbed from the bed. She swung the shutters open filling the room with a blaze of yellow light. A single white cloud was suspended in the azure sky. Below, on the terrace, a couple were eating breakfast.

'Fuck,' Gould said. 'What's the time?'

'Seven thirty.'

'Can't we sleep some more?'

'I'm hungry. I want coffee.'

'Ring room service.'

'They don't have room service here.'

Gould struggled out of bed. 'What was the message?'

'Instructions. She's going to pick me up this afternoon from Gigaro plage, a few miles from here. The house is in the hills. She says it's remote and that there's no phone signal. It's not safe to drive on the forest tracks after dark, so if I'm still there at nightfall she's invited me to stay the night.'

'I'd like to come.'

'No. You'll only distract her.'

'Do you really think that Laura's going to be there?'

'That's what Camille said. That's why she asked me to come

here. And it's an excuse for a short holiday, right? A chance to get to know one another.'

'Am I on probation?'

He lifted her hair and kissed her neck.

She smiled back at him in the mirror.

'So how did you find this place?' he asked.

'On the internet.'

'You haven't been here with someone before?'

'No.'

'Let's have breakfast.'

•

Élodie found a parking place at the side of the beach road, and, as instructed by Camille, walked away from the beach on a path that climbed through the scrub beneath a hillside encrusted with umbrella pines. Élodie could hear the engine of a car. Finally, a yellow open sided Jeep appeared around the bend, its tyres lifting mud and sand.

Camille's eyes were shaded by the brim of a straw hat. 'Jump in,' she called.

Élodie was glad to step out of the sun.

'You found me then,' Camille said.

'Yes.'

'I like your sunglasses.' She took off her hat. 'Let's swap.'

'Okay… if you want. Are you high?'

'High? Of course not.'

Élodie handed Camille her sunglasses and popped the hat onto her head. Camille's blonde fringe and lightly freckled nose made her look very young.

'Ready?' Camille manoeuvred the car around, bashing the bumper on a tree trunk as she did so. 'Don't worry,' she said, 'it's just an old banger.' They sped along the narrow track, climbing into the wood.

'Is this a private road?' Élodie asked.

'Yes. It's owned by the few people who live on this side of the peninsular.'

On the higher ground, the landscape opened out into a pretty mosaic of small vineyards and wooded hillsides. Across the small valley, a villa nestled between the trees. It was clear that the villa occupied a position that meant that it looked both inland and out to sea. From where they were, on the opposite slope of the valley, the Mediterranean's glittering surface could be glimpsed in the far distance.

They drove beside a dried-up riverbed boarded by tall bamboo shoots. 'Does your father own the vineyards?'

'Yes, he owns all of this. Tenants work the estate, though. My dad's a snob. He doesn't care for rosé. In fact, he doesn't like anything about the Var. He rarely comes here.'

'So why have this place?'

'He bought the estate when he was a young man without even seeing it. The idea was to make money. He thought he'd be able to build a hotel and villas. But it's protected, and the local politicians are stubborn. They couldn't be bought. So he did nothing with it for decades. There used to be just a few old farm buildings. A few years ago, he managed to get planning permission for one luxury villa because he had a famous architect who designed something beautiful that fits in with the landscape. You'll see. I like it so much here that I've persuaded him not to sell it. At least for now.'

'Does he own a yacht?'

'Yes. He rarely makes use of it.'

'It's a status symbol?'

'No. It's a money-spinner. He hires it out.'

They had entered the wood on the other side of the valley. The track climbed steeply. It ended at a tall gate of black metal. Camille pressed a button on a gadget and the gate slid slowly open. On the other side, trees lined a gravel drive that ended before a modern building of light brown stone, steel and glass. A bike lay on the gravel.

'I like my solitude,' Camille said as she led Élodie inside. 'The housekeeper only comes once a week. I'm very tidy.'

Élodie felt that she had entered a contemporary art gallery emptied of its exhibits. The large rooms, all painted white, were almost empty. Walls of glass revealed panoramic views in all directions. They were high above the sea and at times Élodie felt as though she was flying over the water. Camille led her through the house to the series of terraces that formed the rear garden. A swimming pool had been cut into the last terrace, the water level with the white flagstones that surrounded it. The pool stretched to the very end of the terrace so that it seemed that the water flowed over the side. Umbrella pines, olive trees and groves of lavender between lines of white gravel formed the garden. On the first terrace, immediately beyond the French windows, a long table was shaded by a canopy that looked like the sail of a ship. An ice bucket rested on the table along with a jar of orange juice and a bowl of olives.

'I thought you might like something to drink and eat,' Camille said. 'I can bring out some cheese and bread.'

'Perhaps later,' Élodie said.

'At least have a glass.' She lifted a bottle of rosé from the ice bucket and filled two glasses. 'It's still cold.'

'Thank you.'

Élodie took a sip of wine. Camille emptied her glass.

'Slow down.'

'I was thirsty. It's so hot. I'm sure you'd love to dive into the pool.'

'I'd rather talk.'

'All right.' Camille sat on the table. She reached for the wine bottle and poured herself another glass. 'How's your policeman? Tom, isn't it? Have you left him in a hotel nearby?'

'I didn't come here to talk about Tom.'

'Perhaps I'll steal him away from you. You don't think I could? I'm ten years younger than you. I'm teasing. I would never do that. But if he just took me it wouldn't be my fault, would it?'

'Camille… Please concentrate.'

'I am.'

'Where's Laura?'

'Laura? Oh, she won't be coming.'

'What's going on, Camille? You asked me to come here to talk to her.'

'It was my father's idea that you should come.'

'Your father? Tell me what's going on?' Élodie said firmly.

'Please let me tell you in my own time.'

'I don't understand.'

'Before I say anything we have to be in the pool.'

'Why?'

'He said so.'

'Who? Your dad?'

'Please…'

'Okay. I don't have a bathing suit.'

'I've put one out for you. It's there.' Camille pointed at a chair. 'We're the same size.'

'Okay.'

'You can leave your bag here.'

•

Élodie swam the length of the pool. At the far end there was a steep drop down to a little cove.

She swam to where Camille was resting against the side of the pool.

'Now will you talk to me?'

'Yes.'

'I'm going to sit on the side. Okay?'

'Okay. I will too.'

Camille sat in the lotus position. She looked down at her feet.

'You said just now that Laura isn't coming. Is that right?'

Camille nodded. 'It's important that you know that I loved my sister. Say that you understand.'

'Yes, I understand.'

'We were two scared little girls when our parents married. We were inseparable back then. But when we were around fourteen Laura started to… At the time I thought that she was being influenced by some of her older friends, that she was growing up too quickly. I was boring and good, always working hard at school. Laura was rebellious. Not because she was seeking adventure, but because she was unhappy and cynical about everything. Well, you get the picture. Even in recent times, though, I loved it when we got together, just the two of us, because then the old Laura would re-emerge.'

Camille fell silent.

'Do you meet here?'

'Yes, this was our place. We would spend the summer together here.'

'So, Laura asked you to pretend that she had disappeared? It was a game the two of you decided to play?'

'No.'

'You were together in York the night she supposedly went missing.'

'Oh, you've worked that out, have you?'

'Is that when you decided? On a whim?'

'No. Laura wasn't in York that night.'

'Okay… So…'

'Will you please let me speak?'

Élodie nodded, and waited.

'When I took up my place at Oxford, I think Laura felt betrayed. She did the silent treatment on me. She didn't even tell me to start with that she had moved to London. But one day she turned up in Oxford. We made up, and had two really lovely days together.'

Élodie waited.

'At the start of the summer I was meant to go to America to study for a few months at NYU, but I changed my mind at the last minute. I came here on my own. I hoped that Laura would be here. I wanted to surprise her. The house was empty so I went out to the terrace. Laura was in the pool with a man. This surprised me because we had an agreement not to bring men here. And yet there she was, having sex with an older man in the pool.'

She looked into Élodie's eyes.

'Do you see where this is going? The man lifted his head away from Laura's neck. It was dad.'

Camille fell silent.

'I'm sorry,' Élodie said.

'I ran back to my car and drove away from the property. I parked between the trees. I thought I was going to pass out. I don't know how long I sat there before the panic went away. I walked to a place on the coastal path that gave a view of our cove. After a while I saw my father leave in a motorboat. I went back to the house.'

'You told Laura what you'd seen?'

'I felt… a terrible grief. She was shameless about what she'd done. She was defending herself, I know that.'

'It's okay,' Élodie said. 'Take your time.'

'She told me that it had been going on since she was fourteen, and that she loved him. She said that he wasn't her real father, so they'd done nothing wrong. We argued.'

'You never suspected?'

'No.' She paused. 'I know what you're thinking. That Laura was abused by him. But I know him, and I know her.'

'I understand why it's easier for you to blame Laura. But you know that she was abused.'

'Don't patronise me. I'm not telling you this because I want your opinion, I'm telling you because I need to tell the truth about what happened next. For a moment we stopped shouting at each other. She was upset by my distress. She tried to embrace me. I shoved her away. We were here beside the pool. I remember that she started to cry. Through her tears she accused me of being jealous. I pushed her too hard. She fell backwards and hit her head. I couldn't wake her.'

Camille looked up at Élodie. 'I can't even cry anymore,' she said.

Élodie touched Camille's arm.

Camille was looking through her. 'I've told her everything, papa.'

Élodie turned and saw Roche standing just a few steps away. Startled, she rose to her feet.

'Keep calm, Élodie. I didn't mean to spook you.'

'I feel better, papa,' Camille said.

'I'm relieved, darling. You see, I was right. You needed to tell. Why don't you go to your room and get some rest?'

'Yes, I do feel tired.'

She stretched out her arms. Roche pulled her to her feet and kissed her on the cheek. She walked away towards the house.

'I feel ambushed,' Élodie said. 'I want to get dressed.'

'Of course. While you do that, I'll organise coffee.'

16

Élodie waited for Roche on the terrace. She reached for her bag. Her phone was missing. She looked up and saw Roche crossing the empty living room. 'Coffee's coming,' he said.

'I don't want a coffee. Where's my phone?'

'I have it.' He took the phone from his pocket and placed it on the table.

'Is that why Camille would only talk at the pool? Because you thought I might record our conversation on my phone, or that I'd be wearing a wire?'

'Yes. I was being very prudent. I didn't really think that you would make a recording. You came here to meet Laura, not to hear Camille's confession. I apologise for the subterfuge. I realised a while ago that Camille needed to tell an official person what had happened; that she wouldn't be able to move on with her life until this happened.'

‘If I go public with this, she’ll deny everything and you’ll accuse me of harassment… Is that right?’

‘Yes. Something like that.’

‘I’d like to leave now,’ she said.

‘Surely we haven’t finished? And anyway, it’s ten kilometres or more to a main road. A long way to walk, especially once it gets dark. I’ve prepared one of the guest rooms for you. If you stay until morning, I’ll drive you.’

‘Tom will come looking for me.’

‘No. He knows you might stay the night.’

‘What are you hoping will happen if I stay?’

‘I only want to give you time to think things through. If you leave now, you’ll spill the beans to Gould and that would not be sensible.’

Élodie thought for a moment. She looked through the panels of glass at the hills and sea, and registered how isolated the house was.

‘I’ll stay if you’ll answer my questions.’

‘Yes, in the context of a conversation over dinner. I’ve brought an assistant who is working away in the kitchen. I have two further conditions. I’ll need to keep your phone while we talk. And, since I’m of a certain generation and value etiquette, I think we should dress for dinner. You’ll find a Dolce and Gabbana cocktail dress laid out on the bed in your room. Why don’t you take time to bathe and rest, and we’ll meet back here in an hour?’

•

'Do you like the dress?' Roche asked Élodie. He indicated that she should sit down on one of the brown leather armchairs in the spacious living room. Élodie looked down at the hem of the dress, and momentarily felt the garment's green lace between her finger and thumb.

'Well, it fits perfectly.'

Roche sat down and crossed his legs. He was wearing a blue suit and a mustard-coloured shirt.

A strong-looking young man with short black hair and a neat beard came into the room.

'This is Paul,' Roche said.

'Good evening, Madame. What would you like to drink?'

'Paul is talented,' Roche said. 'He is both chef and waiter tonight.'

'Please could I have a neat whisky,' Élodie said.

'I'll have the same,' Roche said. 'Laphroaig.'

'Will Camille be joining us?' Élodie asked.

'I hope she will come down later for dinner. But I thought we should spend a little time alone.'

Paul came back with the drinks, and then left the room. 'He has a lot of grace for a big man, no?' Roche said. 'He was seventeen years old, living rough in Marseille and selling drugs when I found him. I gave him a job in one of my restaurants. It was the making of him. Within a few years he had worked his way up to sous-chef.

These days, his main remit is security: he's the best fixer I've ever had. Recently he's been doing a job for me in England.'

Élodie tasted the whisky.

'Let's talk. First, though, I need to take your phone again.'

Élodie handed Roche her phone. He turned it off and placed it in his pocket.

'When I returned to the house, Laura had only just died. If I'd arrived a minute or so earlier…' Roche paused. 'Camille was in a terrible state. It was devastating, but I had to be strong for her.'

Roche paused. 'I'm a little anxious,' he said.

'Where had you gone?'

'The details don't matter. There was nothing I could do for Laura. I think she died instantly. A little shove and she hit her head on the flagstones and that was it.'

'What did you do next?'

'I arranged for Camille to return to Bordeaux.'

'Immediately?'

'Yes, that night. Then I did what was necessary.'

'You disposed of your daughter's body, and cleaned the scene?'

Roche picked up his glass and drank. 'Yes.'

'Was Paul with you?'

'I had trusted employees with me, but I won't tell you their names.'

'Will you tell me where you buried her body?'

'Surely that's obvious.'

'You buried her at sea.'

'Yes. As far as I could, in the most tragic circumstances, I acted with dignity. I was grief-stricken.'

'The dignity of a man who only a few hours before had sex with his daughter in the swimming pool?'

'Is that the aspect that resonates most strongly with you? What a prudish little bourgeoise you are. How could someone like you ever understand?'

'You started to molest your stepdaughter when she was a child. You're damned.'

Roche emptied his glass. 'I waited until she was nearly fifteen in fact. She knew more than enough by then to make her own decisions.' He paused. 'But, you're right to say that I am damned. I knew it was wrong. I just couldn't stop myself. I wanted her, so I took her. And the fact that I loved her as a daughter made it so much more intense for me.'

'What did you tell Camille?'

'I told her the truth, or at least as much as I thought she could handle. I asked her to forgive me. And that's as much as I'm going to tell you about my relationship with my daughters. You'll never understand, let alone accept, the desire that Laura felt for me.'

'Did you tell Camille to impersonate Laura and to travel to York?'

'No. That was Camille's idea. She didn't tell me. It was a mistake. When they were younger, Camille and Laura enjoyed dressing up as each other. Camille has a brown wig. She had Laura's purse and credit cards. In those first days after Laura died,

Camille was terrified that she would go to prison. She came up with a plan to misdirect the authorities, and, to my surprise, it did work. It held up throughout your investigation, but perhaps it was in danger of unravelling?'

'The cameras caught Laura as herself later in the evening boarding a train to London.'

'Ah. But I suspect that only led you to think that both sisters were in York on that day. It was a difficult moment when you showed us a picture of Camille believing it to be of Laura.'

'Did Camille tell you that she was going to send the fake email from Laura?'

'That was my decision. I decided it was time to find some closure.'

'And what about your wife? Are you going to tell her the truth?'

'No. I think she has early dementia.'

'Is she still in the sanatorium?'

'Yes. She's in the Sanatorium Montaigne, so not far from home.' After a pause, he said, 'I hope you decide to stay silent, but if you don't I have a strategy in place.'

'You have a strategy in place? Is that another threat?'

'I'm curious to see what you do next. Part of me would like to play this out. But, I care more about my daughter. Do you believe me?'

'That you care for Camille? Yes.'

'She's in a very fragile state. I want the best solution for her, and I hope you do too.'

'Yes, but…'

'She told you the truth. Did you believe her?'

'Yes.'

'That should be enough.'

'I'll have to tell my colleagues.'

'Why?'

'I won't lie to Tom.'

'You don't need to lie. You just need to tell him that Laura didn't show.'

'I won't let you make me complicit. I'll tell Tom. We'll decide together.'

'It's your choice.'

Camille entered the room from the terrace. She was wearing an elegant black dress.

'Ah, there you are,' Roche said, standing to hug her. 'Thank you for joining us. You look rested.'

'Have you finished talking?'

'Yes.'

Camille glanced at Élodie.

'I told you she wouldn't understand.'

'The important thing is that it has been said. As we agreed, everything has been said.'

'Yes. Do you recognise this little dress, papa?'

'No.'

'Do you think it's pretty?'

'Yes, very.'

'It was Laura's.'

'Okay, my darling… Don't start. Are you going to be all right? You have taken your medication, haven't you?'

She nodded. 'I'll be a good girl. I'm starving. Paul's ready to serve.'

'Shall we eat?' Roche asked Élodie.

'If you like,' Élodie said. 'But afterwards, I'd like to go to bed. And I'd like to leave early tomorrow.'

'As you wish. Paul will drive you.'

•

After Élodie had said goodnight, Roche and Camille sat together for a few minutes on the terrace, and then Camille made her way down the garden paths to the swimming pool. She stepped out of her dress and dived into the water. The pool, illuminated from below, had the green glow of absinthe, and ripples of light played against the surrounding foliage. Camille floated on her back. She stayed so still that Élodie, watching from her second-floor room, thought of a dead girl in a pool. Roche had disappeared. As Camille walked back to the house, she lifted her arms to squeeze water from her hair. Paul, clearing the table, turned away as she strolled by him into the house. After he had finished tidying the terrace, Paul turned off the outside lights and went inside. The pool disappeared.

Élodie stayed awake for a long time, thinking about what Roche had said. The house was so silent that she decided that he must have left. At six o'clock she went downstairs. Paul was waiting in the kitchen, as agreed. 'How did you sleep, Madame?' he asked.

'Fine, thank you. Please can we leave straight away?'

On the short drive to Gigaro, they didn't speak a word.

It was light by the time Élodie arrived back in Gassin. She didn't go up to the room. She sat at one of the tables on the terrace opposite the hotel and watched as the hills turned from grey to green and the sea from violet to blue. The buildings of Sainte Maxime appeared on the other side of the bay. A luxury yacht glided like a shark between a shoal of small boats.

A man and a woman arrived on scooters to open the little foyer and bar of the hotel. Élodie asked for a coffee. She sent Tom a message to say that she was back, and waited for him to come down from the room.

He joined her after twenty minutes. 'So, you stayed the night.'

'Yes.'

'What happened?'

'Laura didn't show.'

'I had a feeling she wouldn't.'

'By the time I gave up on her it was dark and too late for Camille to drive me back.'

'How was Camille?'

'She was okay.'

'She was there alone?'

'The house is quite remote. There are no other properties there.'

'How did you spend the time?'

'We talked. Swam in the pool.'

'What now?'

Élodie paused. 'I think it's time to let Laura Roche go.'

'I think you're right. I've been thinking about the future. I need to break the cord between myself and Becky. I'll ask Brown for unpaid leave.'

'You could spend time in Bordeaux.'

Gould smiled tentatively. 'So you want to keep going?'

She smiled. 'Yes. I want to keep going.'

17

A long drive of pristine white gravel led to the Sanatorium Montaigne. On one side of the complex stood the grand old buildings of a former abbey, including a chapel and cloisters. Opposite, a modern building of glass and concrete was surrounded by the hospital gardens. A small vineyard, as ancient as the abbey, stretched into the wooded hillside.

Élodie parked at the side of the drive and entered the large foyer of the new building. The young woman behind the reception desk smiled and asked Élodie to take a seat. 'I know how this tends to work,' Élodie said, showing her ID card. 'I don't expect to be kept waiting. Tell that to the person you're about to ring.'

A few minutes later a green door slid open and a stocky fair-haired man entered the foyer. He wore the same grey scrubs as the other members of staff. He took hold of Élodie's offered hand, squeezing firmly. Élodie looked through his black framed glasses at his neutral eyes. 'Tomas Richter. I'm the director here. You are?'

'Lieutenant Duquette.'

'You're asking to see Elisabeth Roche?'

'Yes.'

'I'll take you to her.'

'You will?'

'Yes. You're surprised? You were expecting that I'd put up barriers?'

'Well…'

'She's by the lake. We can talk on the way.'

He led Élodie out into the garden.

'We encourage visits because they are normally beneficial, but please can I ask you why you want to see this patient?'

'This is not an official visit. When we were looking for her daughter, I came to know her quite well. I just want to see for myself how she is.'

'She is not well, I'm afraid. Let me put it this way, she is not living in the real world. She can be lucid, but her mind has lost the capacity to recognise even the people she loves. Her condition requires heavy medication.'

'I promise that I'll just sit with her. You can stay if you like.'

'There's no need for that.'

They had reached a manicured lawn. Ahead, the flat surface of a lake emitted a silvery light. A woman was sitting on a bench at the water's edge.

'There she is. I'll leave you now, but if you want to see me afterwards, please do ask for me at the reception desk.'

Élodie approached Elisabeth from one side, so that she wouldn't surprise her. 'Hello.'

Elisabeth looked up from the book she was reading. 'Hello.'

'Is it all right if I sit here?'

'Of course.'

Élodie sat down on the bench. For a moment she looked back at the hospital. The doctor had disappeared. A nurse pushed a patient in a wheelchair across the lawn towards a clump of trees.

Elisabeth smiled. 'It's beautiful here, isn't it? The surface of the lake is like a mirror.'

'Yes. My name's Élodie, Madame Roche. Do you remember me?'

Elisabeth leant towards Élodie a fraction and studied her face. 'Do you work here?'

'No.'

'I'm sorry, I don't know you.'

'I know your daughter.'

'My daughter? You're mistaken. I don't have children.' She smiled. 'And you? You're of childbearing age. I hope you are blessed and you give birth to boys not girls.'

'Why do you say that?'

'It's obvious. Isn't it?'

'Does your husband visit you?'

'My husband died a long time ago. He drove his car into a tree.'

She picked up her book.

'Can I ask... What are you reading?'

'Shakespeare. *Richard II*. In English. I find Shakespeare very comforting, and, besides, I've been asked to play the queen in the little theatre they have here. Will you read the lines with me?'

'Yes, of course.'

Elisabeth handed the book to Élodie. 'You read the part of the queen's maid-in-waiting.'

Élodie rested the book against her knee.

'Don't worry. Just read the lines normally.'

'I'll try. Shall I start?'

'Yes.'

'Madam, we'll dance.'

'My legs can keep no measure in delight, when my poor heart no measure keeps in grief. Therefore, no dancing, girl, some other sport.'

'Madam, we'll tell tales.'

'Of sorrow or of joy?'

'Of either, madam.'

'Of neither, girl. For if of joy, being altogether wanting, it doth remember me the more of sorrow. Or if of grief, being altogether had, it adds more sorrow to my want of joy.'

'Madam, I'll sing.'

'Tis well that thou hast cause, but thou shouldst please me better, wouldst thou weep.'

For a few moments they sat in silence. 'You feel it too?' Elisabeth asked. 'The words are so beautiful.'

Élodie's eyes were moist. 'Yes.'

'And now, if you'll excuse me, I'd like to take a nap.'

'We'll talk again,' Élodie said.

'Oh, I wouldn't book a room at this hotel. You can do much better in Bordeaux.'

As Élodie was crossing the foyer, Richter appeared. 'I hope that wasn't too distressing,' he said.

'Will she get better? Or at least improve?'

He shook his head solemnly. 'There's no cure for dementia. She will only get worse.'

•

The autumn sunlight was warm enough for Brown to light his barbecue. Wearing an apron, and holding a long fork, he watched over the sausages and burgers on the grill. Karen was helping his wife rake up beech leaves and lift them into a wheelbarrow.

Élodie broke away from Bercot and Gould and joined Brown on the patio. 'So, you're still talking to me,' she said.

'What do you mean?'

'Tom's sabbatical.'

'It can't start until next year.'

'That's fine.'

'As long as he comes back.'

Brown poked the blackened sausages with the fork.

'Make sure they're cooked inside,' Élodie said.

'I know what I'm doing,' Brown snapped. 'I've done this hundreds of times and no one's died yet.'

For a few moments she watched Bercot and Gould, amused at their discomfort at being left alone together. Rose, standing a few steps apart, was looking at something on his phone.

'It was thoughtful of you to invite the capitaine today.'

'Toulon are playing Leeds tomorrow. We're going together.'

'You are?'

'You've been here two hours and you haven't mentioned the Roche girl or Brenton. What's wrong with you?'

'Oh, I've drawn a line under it. Finally.'

'It was all much ado about nothing, wasn't it?'

Brown's wife came over to check on the food. Élodie's phone rang. She made her excuses and moved to one side. It was Roche. She hesitated before lifting the phone to her ear. She walked around the side of the house and into the apple orchard.

'Where are you?' Roche asked.

'I'm not telling you.'

'Yorkshire?'

'What do you want?'

Brown's daughter's grey horse was cantering through the hay. The meadow climbed to a row of chestnut trees.

'It was good of you to visit my wife, but you could have told me.'

'I had to see her for myself, to make sure that the dementia is real.'

'Because, otherwise, it would have been your duty to tell her the truth about Laura?'

'Yes.'

'I wonder. I'm sure our paths will cross soon. I very much look forward to seeing you again.'

Roche ended the call before Élodie had time to respond.

'Who was that?'

She turned to see Gould.

'No one. Just work.'

'You and your secrets.'

'What do you mean?'

He smiled. 'Nothing.' He looked at her feet: her flat sandals consisted of only a few leather straps. 'You've wounded me pretty bad,' he said. 'Even your ankles make me hard.'

She smiled and touched his face. 'Of the two of us, I'm not the most secretive,' she said.

He thought for a moment. 'I'm more secret about the past; you're more secret about the present.'

She paused. 'That was Charles Roche.'

'I thought so.'

'How could you tell? I didn't say his name.'

'Because something in the tone of your voice changes when you speak to him. Is he pestering you for sex?'

'I can handle Roche.'

'What really happened at the villa, Élodie?'

She walked away between the apple trees. He followed her bare calves, the skirt of her black linen dress, through the tall meadow grass and weeds. A sudden gust of wind rushed through the branches; its force broke her stride, and she looked over her shoulder to make sure he was following.

She stopped at the gate. The ancient chalk road, open to the harvested fields, brown and bare, stretched to a dip in the landscape. The rolling hills seemed more dust than grass in the fading light.

'Let's not talk about Roche,' she said.

'Fine by me.'

He took hold of the hem of her skirt and pulled her towards him. They stood side by side looking out at the vacant road.

'I came to tell you that the chief's sausages are ready. We should go.'

They walked back to the garden. Brown and his wife were sitting with Bercot at the table. He handed Élodie a glass of red wine.

'Where's Karen and Kevin?' she asked.

'Karen went inside to get another bottle,' Brown said. 'I don't know where Rose went.'

'There's salad as well as hot dogs,' Mrs Brown said. She was facing the French windows. 'Here she is. Oh dear God.'

Élodie turned. The front of Karen's white dress was blood-spattered. Her right hand, dangling against her thigh, was solid red; it held a kitchen knife. Blood dripped from the tip of the blade. The sight momentarily transfixed even the three police officers. 'Oh dear God,' Mrs Brown repeated, her hand covering her mouth.

Tiny freckles of blood covered Karen's expressionless face. She walked across the patio before turning out of sight.

'Bring her back,' Brown told Élodie.

'Mind the knife, though,' Gould said. He ran into the house.

Élodie followed Karen across the yard beside the orchard. She called out her name gently but allowed her to keep walking. She kept her eye on her arm and the knife. Karen walked on, seemingly oblivious to Élodie's presence. When she reached the lane and the open fields, her pace quickened. She looked down and registered the knife clenched in her fist and the trail of blood in the white dust. She dropped the knife. Élodie moved forward and pulled Karen into an embrace.

Élodie eased Karen down onto the grass verge. Her phone bleeped. 'Rose is dead,' Gould said. 'She stabbed him in the heart and throat. The kitchen floor is a lake of blood. Do you have her?'

'Yes.'

'Shall I come and help?'

'No. We're just sitting.'

'Why did she do it?'

'I don't know yet. Give me a moment, Tom.'

'We've called it in so you don't have long.'

'How is the chief?'

'He's not saying much at the moment.'

Karen was looking at her hand. The blood was already starting to dry. 'I'm sorry,' she said. 'He's dead?'

'Yes. You need to tell me everything before we go back.'

‘Can I take off this dress? Can I wash?’

‘You know you can’t.’

‘He came to my house…’

Élodie waited. She placed a stray strand of Karen’s hair behind her ear. They sat side by side at the edge of the white road.

‘When did he come to your house?’

‘Just before I went off sick. Do you remember?’

‘Yes. Did you invite him?’

‘No. I was in the bath. He broke in and pushed my head under the water, and then he pulled me out of the tub by my hair. He placed a plastic bag over my head and carried me into my bedroom. I started to suffocate. At the last moment he ripped the bag. He forced my head up and poured a bottle of vodka down my throat.’

Karen paused and looked into Élodie’s eyes.

‘Do you believe me?’

‘Yes, I believe you.’

‘I was lying naked on the bed. He took pictures. He said things to me. I was retching and close to passing out. I don’t know what he said, but he was threatening me and laughing. He made himself something to eat before leaving my house.’

‘Did he rape you?’

‘No. Are people going to think what he did wasn’t serious because of that?’

‘No. It was a savage assault that could have killed you, and it was sexual. He violated you.’

'Thank you.'

'I know the answer, but I have to ask you… Were you ever intimate with him?'

'Never.'

'Did you reject him?'

'No. He never tried. He liked to boss me, and I wouldn't cower. We argued. I think this enraged him.'

'He was a bully of women.'

Dusk had fallen rapidly, and the hills were darkening. The road was a white gash. Far below a pulsing blue light could be seen.

'It's the car,' Élodie said. 'We don't have long.'

'You're wondering why I didn't report it,' Karen said.

'I'm not. I know why you didn't report it. He would have said you had consensual sex. He planned the assault very carefully.'

'Anyway, I felt ashamed.'

'You didn't do anything wrong.'

'What will happen to me? The chief won't understand. Tom won't understand.'

'I wouldn't be so sure of that.'

'The chief invited Rose here today, didn't he?'

Élodie waited, and then said, 'What happened in the kitchen?'

'He followed me in there. He came up behind me so that I could feel his breath on my neck. He started to mock me. He said he could do whatever he wanted with me. The knife must have been on the surface. I picked it up, turned and stabbed him. I just… snapped.'

'He didn't do anything physical?'

'No.'

Élodie paused. 'When you make your statement, say that he grabbed you and sexually assaulted you. Okay?'

Karen nodded. Gould, Brown and Bercot were at the gate. 'I can't face him,' Karen said.

'Just wait here a moment,' Élodie told Karen.

She left Karen and walked over to the others.

'We were worried,' Gould said.

'Why did she do it?' Brown said. Élodie registered the desolation in his eyes as he looked at Karen.

'Rose assaulted her, it was why she went off sick.' She quickly recounted the details.

'And you believe her?' Brown asked.

'Don't do that. She's going to get plenty of that when this gets to trial. She needs your support.'

'I had to ask, Élodie.'

'It's partly my fault,' Gould said. 'She asked to be partnered with someone else. I knew there were issues. I brushed them off. I told her to toughen up.'

'You couldn't have known,' Élodie said.

'I should have listened to her.'

'Damn right you should have listened to her,' Brown snapped.

'Shouting is not going to help,' Élodie said.

'I don't understand how she could lose her reason like that,' Brown said. He opened the gate. 'Karen,' he called. 'Come here.'

Karen looked over. She shook her head.

Élodie touched Brown's arm, as if to hold him back, but Brown ignored the gesture and walked quickly down the track until he was standing in front of Karen.

'I'm sorry, sir,' she said.

Brown pulled her up into his arms. 'It's going to be all right,' he said.

THE AUTHOR

Simon Trowbridge was born in Oxford, England, in 1961. He was educated at Wallingford School, King's College, London, and University College, London. He is the author of a biography of Jean-Philippe Rameau and a history of the Comédie-Française.

www.ingramcontent.com/pod-product-compliance
Lightning Source LLC
Chambersburg PA
CBHW030544310726
48979CB00010B/2029/J

* 9 7 8 1 9 9 9 7 3 0 5 4 3 *